DEAD HOPE

JACK ZOMBIE #2

FLINT MAXWELL

Special thanks to Sabrina Roote

The author greatly appreciates you taking the time to read his work.

For Savanna,

the female version of Norm

People say that where there's life, there's hope, and I have no quarrel with that, but I also believe the reverse.

There is hope, therefore I live.

— Stephen King, *Revival*

1

It's been six months since we left Woodhaven, and I don't want to remember any of it — the chaos, the dead friends, the enemies, or the pain. But I know I'll never forget. Never truly forget. Every part of this crumbling world is a reminder.

We haven't stopped traveling, haven't stopped searching for a new home. It's been three days since we've seen a working car. We sleep in Norm's Jeep, back seats down, no blanket, no pillow besides our hands. One of us keeps watch, Norm's big gun or the Glock I pulled off a dead police officer from a town called Paris nearby.

Those not infected by this disease have taken to looting, running, and hiding. My group is no different. We do what we have to do to survive.

We have to.

I am on watch this morning. The sun rises in a bloody, red haze. There's fog outside of the window, almost no visibility. It's as thick as the darkness that came before it, but I am not as scared as I used to be on these watches. Mainly, I'm tired. Mainly, I'm fed up. Fed up because the way we live is not life. I'm tired of having to watch my back, having to make sure no one does anything stupid. I'm tired of scavenging for my food like a caveman. I'm tired, just too damn tired.

We are parked off some country road in a field, never too far from the pavement. Most of the dead are not out here. Mostly, they are in the big cities, like Indianapolis and Chicago. Each day we have a goal. Something small like get food, find gas, find medicine, find shelter. Sometimes we fail. Sometimes we succeed.

The long term goal has been to find Eden. We are so close.

I just hope Eden is not a myth. I hope it's real. For all of our sakes.

I take a few deep breaths to calm myself. Behind me, the light snores of Abby, Darlene, and Norm drone on intermittently. That in itself is calming, knowing my friends, my family, are still alive.

We first heard of Eden outside of Chicago. From a man who'd signed his death certificate not long before we stumbled upon him. He had been shot in the gut, and left for the crows, but I think the zombies would have gotten to him first if we hadn't.

Norm slowed the Jeep to a crawl when we saw his signal. In the empty road, painted in blood-red was the word HELP. There was a trail from the end of the P, and at the end of the trail laid a man named Richard. His face was swollen, black and blue. He'd been shot twice, once in the stomach and once in the shoulder. His wounds were already festering, the flies and the maggots surely not far off.

"What happened?" I asked him.

He didn't ask for help. He didn't cry or scream for God. He just smiled.

"The End happened. It came fast, too, took society with it. All sense of right and wrong."

The man spoke true. It did come fast, almost in the blink of an eye. There's an old saying: Your life can turn on a dime. I never fully understood that saying until I watched our society fall. It toppled over like dominoes, each major city ravaged and ransacked, too fucked for the government to implement quarantines or blockades. I remember hearing about Los Angeles, how it was so overrun, they had to drop bombs on the city. Then it was D.C., New York, Dallas....everywhere. So yeah, The End happened, all right.

But that's not what we wanted to know.

"What happened to *you*?" Norm asked.

Darlene buried her face into my shoulder. Abby

stood as still as a deer about to be mowed down by a semi.

"Couple young men like yourself took what I had, shot me, left me for dead. That's the short of it. Said they were going to a place called Eden. A place where it's safe. I laughed at them. Maybe I shouldn't have done that, but sometimes an old man can't help himself. *Nowhere* is safe."

He pulled his shirt up, completely soaked through with blood, and showed me his wounds. I remember gagging.

"Little did they know they did me a favor," Richard said. I remembered getting a bitter taste in my mouth because there is always hope. Even if the world has gone to shit, there is still hope.

Now, my hope is dwindling.

Norm and I took Abby and Darlene aside, and Darlene asked if there was any way to help him. I knew there wasn't. The only way to help him was to put him down, put him out of his misery, forget about it, and move on. But I couldn't say it.

Luckily, Norm could.

He patted the Magnum on his hip. "Yeah, darling."

"No," Darlene said. "No, we can't do that. We aren't *murderers.*"

"Would you call a vet who sticks a death-needle into a sick dog a murderer?"

Darlene didn't answer, but eyed my older brother as if she hated him.

"Yeah, thought not," Norm said. He looked to me, then to Abby. "All settled then?"

"You can't!" Darlene shouted.

I put my hand on her arm, and gave her a solemn nod.

"It'd be worse of us to just leave him here, Darlene. He'd suffer. We can't let him suffer," I said.

"Always the brains of the family," Norm said. "Guess it's settled." He turned to head back to the side of the road where a man named Richard slowly bled out from multiple gunshot wounds.

"Wait," I said. "Let me do it."

Norm gave me a half-smile as if he was both proud and a little unsettled. "All right, little brother." He handed me the Magnum. I took it and I swear it never felt heavier than it did in that moment. The deaths before all of this, those had been justified. Pat Huber was a murderer, his son was a zombie. This? Well, this was a first step into a very dark world.

I went over to Richard, my legs quivering, my arm feeling like it held a fifty-pound dumbbell in hand. He looked up at me as I aimed the barrel at his head. The waning sun illuminated the dried blood on the corners of his mouth. "Thank you," he said and closed his eyes.

I closed my own eyes, felt the trigger brush up

against my finger. That bad taste invaded my mouth again.

Richard had begun praying, his lips moving fast, his eyes still closed. I couldn't catch the words, just a series of hisses. The gun shook violently in my hand. I couldn't do it. I could not kill a man who I didn't know deserved to die. I let the gun fall and began to turn, but Norm was there as he was in Woodhaven. He took the Magnum out of my grip, gave me an understanding nod. I couldn't even watch. I turned my back to the scene, looking at Darlene and Abby across the way, and when the gun clapped, my eyes didn't even blink.

Norm shot him in the head. I remember hearing the echo of the gun in the dead town down the road, then I remember the thud of his body hitting the grass.

Norm and I buried him under some big rocks and a fallen log so the dead couldn't get to him.

Sometimes I wonder if Richard had the right idea. Maybe nowhere is safe anymore, maybe dying was a blessing more than a curse. It's one of those questions philosophers of this time will ponder for as long as the dead don't eat them, I guess.

I wonder about that question now as I gaze through the window.

I see a glint of yellow, something like a dim flashlight winking on and off in the fog about fifty feet in front of the Jeep, but that's all I see, and it's all I need to see to know what it is.

It's one of *them*. The big Z word. Zombie, Dead, Infected, Deadhead, Pus-bag, and on and on.

They are the only ones with eyes like that.

I tighten my grip on the gun. Our ammo is sparse, the thunderclap of the weapon only draws more of them, but if I have no other choice, I will blast this thing to kingdom come.

The engine is not running. The lights are not on. It has no reason to come this way other than out of sheer curiosity.

I slink lower in the seat until my eyes are barely visible over the dashboard. The yellow glow disappears. It might've turned around, might be going the other direction.

The second time we heard of Eden was in Kentucky. We were in a small town with a name I can't remember — something that ended in 'ville,' and not Louisville. The power was still on in this town. This was before *The End* really took on its full meaning, when the government was still trying to do something about the spread, before the military was completely overrun, before the President and his cabinet were moved to some bunker miles underground — as if it matters anymore, whenever this disease runs its course, the world leaders will be the leaders of nothing but mass graves. But I think they will — or have already — become a part of those graves.

We left Woodhaven without much of a plan. We

stopped in Indiana en route to Chicago, where Norm lived. Indiana was lost. Not just Indianapolis, but the whole state. So was Chicago, my 65 inch flatscreen, my Honda CR-V, my collection of mint condition, first edition King hardbacks. Lost. The world, lost. Us, lost.

Whatever they cooked up in the lab at the Leering Research Facility was potent. In six months, last I heard, it had spread across the entire world. Pat Huber was right about one thing. The disease was like wildfire and it wouldn't stop until it consumed everything in its path. Believe me, they tried to stop it. North America was basically one large headstone. The country is mostly dark. The power plants don't run without living bodies operating them. The planes don't fly. The cars sit in the middle of the road, bumper to bumper, collecting dust. Money means nothing. Food is already getting hard to come by. They tried quarantines, cures, military involvement, but none of that worked. By the time international travel was banned, the United Kingdom was a mass graveyard. France had been in such a huge zombie war, they'd detonated bombs near the Eiffel Tower and it actually collapsed. I saw a photo before the internet went down. It was chilling.

Of course, we weren't as stupid as some of the other countries. Rumor had it that North Korea dropped atomic bombs on themselves in an attempt to stop the disease from spreading. Their population is now close to zero, and the neighboring nations have been covered in their ashes. South America is sinking — at least that's what a young man told me in Chicago. Whatever the hell that means. Some people we've met on our travels talked of going to Antarctica. Stupid. Another one told me that the fighting near the San Andreas Fault in California had caused the whole damn state to break off and float to Hawaii. I didn't tell Darlene that one, with her sister in San Francisco.

In Kentucky, we saw the sign written on the roof of a barn. It was painted in a shocking white:

GONE TO EDEN. OUTSIDE OF SHARON, FL. SAFE. HAPPY. JOIN US!

This was almost three weeks after we met Richard on the side of the road. None of us had thought of Eden since then. We mostly just thought of survival. There's a stat in advertising I remember learning in one of my college classes that states you have to see an ad seven times for a customer to actually buy your product. I call bullshit on that because I'd heard about Eden only twice and it was already tattooed on my brain. *Twice*. As we got closer, I heard about it more.

And after a few stints in places not so overrun by the dead or choked up by perpetually stopped traffic, we had decided, like the birds, to head south for the winter, and nothing sounded as good as Florida in that moment.

"Why does it have to be fog?" I mutter to myself. "Anything but fog."

Behind me, Norm twitches. His head points toward the dashboard while Abby and Darlene's are near the back windshield. He thinks he's being gentlemanly, but really I don't think either of the ladies care.

"What?" Norm says.

I don't know if he's talking to me or if he's suffering from one of the vivid dreams he so often has. Two tours in Iraq and a man can come back entirely different. So far, Norm's been all right. Sometimes he vies for power. Sometimes he shouts, *"My Jeep, my rules!"* when we disagree with the route he's taken to our next destination. *"If you want to go that way then you can walk!"* is another popular one, but mostly Norm is all right. Much better than I remember him being when we were younger and still living with Mother. And, if I'm being totally honest, it's nice to have my older brother back.

"What is it, Jack?" Norm says.

I turn toward him, seeing the sleep in his eyes.

"You already know," I whisper. I don't want to disturb the girls.

"Already?" He sighs. "Can life get any shittier?"

I could answer, but we both know what it would be. It's a resounding yes. Life can always get shittier when the dead have risen and are out for human flesh.

They were calling it *The End* before we lost touch

with the outside world, before the radio turned to nothing but static and religious babble, before the internet went down, before the twenty-four hour news networks lost their hosts and correspondents to this sickness.

The End.

I'm determined to not let that be the case. I'll look at Darlene, get lost in her eyes, and I'll think to myself, I never want that to end. I will do what I have to do to make this a new beginning.

Anything but *The End.*

"How many?" Norm asks.

I blink blearily. Lack of sleep is catching up to me. I can't remember if I saw one set of those yellow eyes or two. I close my own, lean forward until my forehead rests against the rear sight of the Glock — rear sight is one of the words Norm has taught me since we've been on the road. "One," I say, almost completely sure of myself.

Norm is no dummy. He reads my hesitation. "Shit," he says. "One, two, or three. Doesn't matter as long as it's not a pack." He pulls himself up, pats me on the shoulder. "You need to get some sleep, little bro." He crawls into the driver's seat. Next thing I know, he's got a hand full of metal. It's the big gun he greeted me with back at the Woodhaven Motel, the one Dirty Harry would carry around.

"What are you doing?" I ask. My voice is harsh.

Abby stirs, murmurs something in her sleep.

"I'm taking care of our little pal," he says.

"He's gone," I say. "Let him go. We only kill when we have to."

It's not worth dying over. We are completely safe in the Jeep. We have the upper-hand. Killing one — just *one* — does nothing.

Norm shakes his head. He pulls out the weapons he has in a small bag under his seat. These are the weapons which make no noise, which bring no attention to us. The hammer, the machete, the baseball bat, the tire iron. He pulls the bat out. The wood is chipped and stained a dull red. It's only been six months, but Norm has gotten a lot of mileage out of it. The door opens and the dashboard dings. We have set the overhead light to not come on when the door opens, a lesson we learned the hard way back in Atlanta.

"Seriously, Norm, let it go," I say.

"Nuh-uh," he says. "We are too close to blow it now. I let this one go and next thing you know, it's taking a bite out of my dick while I'm pissin in the woods. You stay here, keep the girls safe."

I almost laughed. The girls don't need protection as long as Abby is around. She has since become quite the killer of the dead. She no longer fears, and I think that's the first step to surviving in this world.

Me, well, I'm constantly scared shitless. I just try

not to show it, mainly for Darlene. Because she worries enough as it is. She doesn't need to know her fiancé is worthless on top of everything else. I love her, but love doesn't bash in zombie brains.

Norm points through the windshield. "There's the son of a bitch," he says. "I'll be back before you can say bacon and eggs."

"Bacon and eggs, asshole," I say.

He glares at me. "Clever, Jack. Always clever." He gets out.

I watch as the fog swallows him up, and thirty seconds later, I'm shaking Abby awake and handing her the Glock. "I'm going to cover Norm," I say, then I pull the machete free from the bag. I may be terrified, but I can't let my older brother go out there alone, even if he *can* handle it.

2

"Norm," I whisper, "come back, you dummy. It's not worth it."

I'm hunched down, a few feet from the Jeep. The fog is thicker outside. I try to think back to where we were last night, the layout of the land. It was a field, what once might've been prime farmland before all this shit happened. Norm parked near the tree line. The dead never seem to wonder out this far in the sticks, away from civilization, but the living do. Sometimes, we have to fear the living more than we fear the dead. Another lesson we had learned the hard way.

"Norm?" I say again, this time louder.

There is no answer. The world is quiet. Not even the bugs buzz or the birds chirp.

I hear a grunt, a soft scream. Wood clunks against a

skull. It causes me to snap my head in the direction of the noise, but it comes from nowhere and everywhere at the same time. I don't know if I'm looking north or south, east or west.

I walk on, the machete leading me at a low angle, a precautionary measure. I don't want to end up shish-kebabing Norm.

"...take that...you...piece of...shit," he says. I see a flash of wood. A flash of blood. Brains.

The thing's eyes no longer blaze yellow. Now, they are dying, the fire inside of them going out.

"I told you to stay in the car," Norm says.

"When did I ever listen to you?" I reply.

"I didn't need your help. It was just one. I could handle it." Norm's face is a blur. I can barely see the machete in front of me let alone him.

"Better safe than sorry," I say. Besides, it's almost never *just one.* They travel in packs, like ravenous animals.

"C'mon, let's get the hell out of here. We should be at Eden by the time the sun goes down. I can't wait another day."

He walks past me, leaving a thin line in the fog, thinner than the one he would've left six months ago. We are all suffering from this life on the run. Sleeping in a crammed Jeep, eating processed foods, drinking warm water and soda. Running. Killing. Sometimes I think it would be easier being one of the monsters, aimlessly shambling about looking for food, moaning, groaning. I realize this would mean giving up. I don't want to give up. If there's one thing I can take from my strained relationship with my mother and brother, it's never give up.

I follow after Norm, heading back to the car. We will probably sleep for another hour or two, then hit the road and look for food and signs of Eden. I know we are close, I can feel it. I even dream about it. In my dreams, the walls are a hundred feet tall. There's electricity and running water that is always hot. I never have to pick up a gun again, I never have to bash in someone's head who might've once been a father or a mother or a priest. Then, of course, I wake up. These last few nights I've woken up to Darlene's quiet sobs. She cries for a sister in San Francisco, a mom and dad in Milwaukee. I don't know what else I can do to comfort her. Darlene is a realist, she knows the chances of their survival are slim, but I pray for them every night. I pray for her. For me. For the whole world. And I'm not even religious.

"Norm," I whisper.

The fog has begun to clear up the slightest bit. I see the outline of the Jeep, its boxy, black shape. I don't see Norm, and luckily, the machete is by my side because I bump into his back.

He has stopped in the middle of the field, and he is not holding his baseball bat any longer. That is in the tall grass, lost somewhere. No. Norm is pointing his gun. It all hits me at this moment: the thumps of their rotting hands against the metal and glass, the gurgling moans, and the screams.

The yellow eyes flicker on and off like lightning bugs as they shamble about. There are at least ten of them.

I grab Norm's arm. He is rigid yet shaking. If I could see his face, I would see a wild mixture of fear and excitement. "Don't shoot," I say. "Abby will handle it."

And sure enough, Abby does.

The Jeep's engine roars to life, the lights turn on, barely visibly through the fog. She doesn't stomp on the gas. She just eases it, and the lights grow brighter as she comes toward us. Instinctively, I back up. When I bump into something, my heart nearly explodes, the adrenaline and fear bursting out of me. I turn around, raising the machete. Six months ago, I would've swung, buried the blade into whatever was behind me, man or dead man. Now, I don't. I don't want the blood on my hands. There are few survivors of this plague or reckoning or whatever the hell this is, and the thought of accidentally killing someone who isn't already dead sickens me. There may come a time when I'm wrong, when I should've swung first, asked questions later, but it's not now.

This time, my enemy, the thing that spooks me is a

tree, one seeming to stretch into the clouds, as old as Time itself. Way to go, Jack.

I turn back around as I hear the sound of the revving Jeep. Abby has sped up. The lights bump and jump as she goes over the uneven landscape. It is coming right for Norm and me.

"We gotta move," I say to Norm.

But he doesn't. He is waving his hands, "Stop! No!"

Somehow, he knows his surroundings, knows we are right by the tree line even in the fog. I think it's some kind of sixth sense he gets from being a former Army grunt. Either that, or he's just a crazy son of a bitch.

Abby doesn't stop. In fact, she speeds up.

I dive out of the way, throwing the machete, knowing I just might've signed my own death certificate because I won't find it in this tickling, tall grass, but if the Jeep rolls me over and breaks my legs or straight-up kills me, then I'm even worse off.

Behind me, at least I think it's behind me, it's the Jeep versus a centuries old tree. By the sound of the glass breaking, metal screeching, I think it's safe to say the tree has won. I glance to my right where I see the faint glow of the red brake lights, and about fifty feet away the group of dead walking toward the crashed Jeep.

This is when the engine cuts off. I hear something

whistle and exhale a great burst of pressure, then all is quiet except for the snarls of the monsters.

I stand up. Surprisingly, my foot knocks into something in the grass. I pick it up. It's the machete. I raise it above my head like a sword.

I told you it's never *just one.*

3

The fog has cleared enough for me to make out their faces. They have been dead a long time. They are squishy, runny. Most of their skin has rotted off to the point of determining whether they're male or female damn near impossible. It doesn't matter. My machete comes for their head regardless of sex, race, age, or occupation. I am a regular open-minded killer of the dead. New Age Slayer is what I call it. If you're already dead and you're still walking, and you have a hankering for human flesh — especially *my* human flesh — then I will defend myself. Plain and simple.

A man wearing overalls and still carrying most of his weight in his middle lunges at me first. His teeth have been rotten longer than he has, that's for sure. I jab the machete at him. This is another lesson I've learned the hard way. One time, as I swung down on a creep like I was a medieval executioner, the blade lodged in her head. I am not strong. I am a string bean and the force of my swing was not enough to reach the creep's brain. She kept coming, kept snapping her jaws at me like one of those chattering teeth toys. Darlene had to help me that time, and she is not too fond of killing these things. It's too messy.

So Overalls is soft enough that I don't need much force. It's in and out like a thumbtack popping a balloon. He drops, all four-hundred pounds of him, into a heap. As he hits, his guts deflate. A wave of black, inky blood douses the tall grass. Six months ago, I might've lost my lunch seeing that but not now.

Next in line is something more akin to a skeleton wearing a dress that might've once been something you put on for church — Sunday's finest is what you'd call it — before *The End.* I raise my leg and kick her in the sternum. I'm practically kicking thin air. Her arms flail out as she stumbles backward, a dusty groan escaping her mouth. In less than two seconds, my machete, still slick with Overalls's brains, collapses her cranium.

"Want more?" I shout to the surrounding dead, my arms out like I'm Russell Crowe in *Gladiator* (minus fifty pounds of muscle). "Come on!"

Their glowing eyes seem to flicker in the fog. Behind me, I hear Norm's grunts, the sounds of his baseball bat clobbering their heads. It's a good sign.

When Norm is locked in the zone, he's like Barry Bonds out there. Each crush of his baseball bat is a home run.

The fog dissipates, showing the dead in all of their disgusting beauty. Lumps, knobs, bones sticking out of fleshy and unusable arms, tattered clothes, melted skin. I'd be lying if I said my stomach isn't clenching.

"Jack!" someone says. I instantly recognize the voice, even through the Jeep's glass. It's Darlene. I risk a glance at the crashed vehicle. Most of the windows are intact except for a large crack through the windshield. The glass is tinted. I can barely make out the white moon of her face, the distressed look in her eyes. "Jack!" She beats on the window as if to break it. She's trapped in the car, surrounded by death, and it's up to me to bust her out.

The dead stream out from the woods. Locusts of the Plague, of the Apocalypse, come to pick the bones clean of all Earth's sinners.

I am frozen, the weight of the situation pressing down on me. I have to save Darlene.

Norm's gun cracks. Two quick shots. Two lightning flashes. Deafening booms. I see a spray of blood. We are getting overrun. When he drops the bat and picks up the Magnum, I know things have taken a turn for the worst.

Shit.

Something grips at my shoulder, causing me to

jump. I turn back around, unfrozen, and I'm face to face with a young man who has died young and will always be young, even as time goes on. That is, until I shove my machete under his chin, poking a hole in the top of his head where a lava burst of scrambled brains spew out and roll down the sides of his face. The light in his eyes immediately fizzles out. I pull the blade free as easily as I lodged it in his head. The next swing decapitates an old woman. Her head rolls off in the grass, mouth missing lips, dentures chomping nothing but air. I stomp on her head, ending that freak show fast.

Darlene, I think. *Gotta to get to Darlene.*

Norm shoots two more times.

"Jack, come on!" it's Abby. She's on top of the Jeep, pointing the Glock at me. She shoots twice and two of the dead fall.

I, with the help of Abby, have cleared a path to the car where the back of Darlene's head is pressed up against the window facing me. I run to the Jeep, throw open the door. She tumbles out, but I catch her.

She's crying. I hate when she cries. The only way I can get her to stop is by taking her into my arms and kissing every inch of her face. But certain circumstances do not let that happen. The real problem is when Darlene is frightened, when she cries, she freezes. And in this world, that's a certain death sentence.

"Go, Darlene!" I shout. "Run."

She takes one look at the dead piled up, making a body-shaped path through this abandoned field, and her eyes widen in terror. A bald corpse in nothing but his underwear sees us, and lumbers away from the crumpled hood of the Jeep. I give Darlene a little push, nothing terrible or violent, just something to get her engine primed and ready to go. She takes off, clumsily but fast. Abby jumps off the roof of the Jeep, and in mid-jump, puts a bullet through the eye of the underwear-wearing corpse. His head jolts back and he stumbles over the tree's root, gone to the fog.

"I got her," Abby says as she lands. She's a thin thing, thinner since all of this shit went down, so I don't hear her land. The Glock looks like it weighs more than her.

I point to the road on the far side of the field. There's a small pond shimmering in the morning sunshine. "Get to the lake! I'll get Norm and the weapons," I say. I didn't even think to say these words. We always know living with the dead means our lives can take a turn for the worst at any moment. We prepare for this stuff. It's almost a reflex. Second nature.

I lunge into the Jeep. Through the tinted glass, I see Norm. A group of the dead surround him, closing in on him, slowly backing him up against the driver's side door. He has the smoking Magnum in one hand, the baseball bat in his other. His gray shirt, already dingy with months on the road, is soaked through with sweat. I reach in the Jeep where our gym bag of weapons sit on the front seat, grab it and pull it out. The dead around the front of the car haven't noticed me.

Norm shoots one in the face, stripping it of its left side. It falls in a bloody spray.

My hand finds the door handle of the back seat. I push it open with a grunt. It's not easy. The Jeep's doors are heavy, and like I said, I'm a weakling.

"Norm! Let's go!"

He looks at me, this crazy look is in his eyes, like he's going to try to take all of them on by himself. Believe me, he probably could, but I love my older brother and I'm not going to let him do something stupid. The baseball bat swings, cracks a short, fat guy on the top of the head. Norm raises the bat again, but my voice stops him mid-strike. "Norm, I can't do this without you."

He looks at me, and the crazy mask he is wearing vanishes.

"I've gone my whole life without you, man. I can't lose you again."

Blood speckles his uneven beard, his forehead, and almost the entire front of his shirt.

"Come on!" I shout.

The crazy look invades his features again. He

squares up to me, raises his weapon. My mouth opens in a protest, something like *Please, don't shoot,* but it's lost in the sound of the gunshot. The glass behind my head shatters, showers over my hands which are laced against the back of my neck. I slowly turn, my heartbeat pounding in my chest. A corpse lays in the grass a mere foot away from where my legs hang out of the Jeep. Its head is a mess of blood and brains and bits of bone. I turn back to Norm as he crawls over the backseats. "Thanks," I say.

"Don't mention it," he says, a smile on his face.

Then we are out of the car and running toward the pond, where Abby and Darlene are little specks on the horizon, barely visible through the now vanishing fog.

4

WE REGROUP AT THE POND. DEAD FISH FLOAT BELLY UP near the surface. Darlene watches them as if they are hypnotizing. I squeeze her hand and say, "It's okay," even though I know I'm lying.

It's not okay. We have just lost the car and barely survived. I think about maybe going back there when the fog clears, but there are too many zombies and the car crashed into that old tree pretty hard.

So we march on.

As the sun slowly burns us overhead, we spend much of the day walking, but I am tired come a couple hours past noon. I don't know the exact time, I just know it's time to rest. I haven't slept in almost twenty-four hours. If I take the watch during the middle of the night, I usually sprawl out in the back of Norm's Jeep while one of the others drives.

But we are so close to Eden I could practically smell the orange groves and taste the clean, *alive* air. Or so that's the image in my head from the countless nights I've dreamed of the place.

Norm looks over his shoulders at me. I'm walking gingerly as if I'm maneuvering through landmines, the bag of weapons hanging off my shoulders and my machete in hand. His face goes from pissed-off to brotherly concern in a matter of seconds. Abby and Darlene follow his gaze.

I must look pretty bad because even Abby looks worried, and lately, nothing worries Abby.

Darlene stops, her shoes breaking a twig that sounds much louder in my head than it actually is, then she's on me.

"Oh, Jack," she says. "Are you feeling all right?" The back of her hand goes up to my forehead, feeling for a fever. I'm not sick, it's just hot outside. Florida weather is nothing like Ohio weather. My shirt sticks to my sweaty skin, there's moisture trickling down the back of my neck. It's not the wheels and mobility of Norm's Jeep that I miss now; it's the air conditioning. God, I'd kill for some air conditioning.

"I'm okay," I say. "Don't worry, let's keep going. Gotta get to Eden today." Even I can hear how weak I sound.

Darlene grips my hand and squeezes. "Let me take the bag. I can carry it, Jack."

She'll have to be carrying me pretty soon.

"You sure you don't wanna rest, little brother? Take a break, maybe a nap. Eight hour power nap, yeah?"

"No," I say. "I'm fine. Gotta get to Eden before sundown."

Though we left the zombies behind in the field, we are never safe. When the sun goes down and their yellow eyes glow viciously with hunger and rage, you do not want to be caught around a horde. If we stop now, who knows how long we'll be walking after dark? I can't have that. I must keep this group safe, I must keep Darlene safe.

But my body says otherwise.

We go on for another half-hour, walking along a long stretch of road. In the distance, I see the varying ups and downs, the farmland next to it, and much, much farther, I see a town. I know it's actually not that far, it's just my tired eyes playing tricks on me. Still, this realization doesn't help me much.

I seem to stare straight ahead for hours.

None of us talk. There's a time and a place for talking and it's not now, can't let any dormant dead things in the surrounding forest know where we are.

The sun is halfway down as Norm turns around to look at me. Him and Abby are about a hundred feet ahead of Darlene and I.

I look up to the sky, sarcastically thinking *Wow, time flies when you're having fun.*

I'm not too out of it to know it's nowhere close to nine in the evening. The darkness overhead is a storm brewing. Gray and black clouds swell, pregnant with rain and thunder and lightning. We will have no choice but to find cover. It looks like it's going to be a hard one, too.

Norm points to a farmhouse. It's on a stretch of farmland which hasn't been farmed in the better part of a year. Beyond this wooden fence that runs the length of the balding patch of land, crops litter the field like trash, looking as unenthused as I feel. The farmhouse is a squat two-story building. Its red brick chimney sticks up into the air like a middle finger. The roof is also red, though I don't think that was its original color. Maybe brown or black. Age and muggy weather have made it rusty, and now it's the color of the chimney. The lawn is overgrown. There's a bicycle leaning up against the porch with its handlebars turned at a neck-breaking angle, grass threatening to swallow it up. But beyond this, there is a large tree with all of its leaves. It's the most alive thing I've seen in a long time. It is a beautiful tree.

Darlene shudders next to me. "Creepy," she says.

"Yeah," Abby agrees.

They must not notice the tree.

"Don't get too comfortable," Norm says, a sarcastic smile on his face. "We're only staying until we all get rested, then we're back on the road. Who knows?

Maybe the previous owners of this place left us a car or some honest-to-God food. I'm sick of eating old Twinkie's and stale potato chips."

"And bugs, don't forget bugs," Abby says, a disgusted look on her face.

Yeah, Norm has been eating bugs. It was a habit he picked up in his military travels. Some foreign country or other where dinner's main course is grasshopper soup and eating beef, pork, or chicken is frowned upon. I won't knock it, but I won't try it, either. I understand where he's coming from. We haven't had meat in a while, and men need their meat. During the fall of American civilization, when there were more people than zombies (this was just a very short time, looking back) you could still find a pound or two of frozen hamburger, chicken breasts, a nice pot roast. Cook them over a fire, get some buns, barbecue sauce or ketchup and mustard, and enjoy. But now, every working freezer has probably stopped.

So yeah, a man needs his meat, even if it is bug meat, and Florida has *a lot* of bugs.

"Hey, if you guys ate some once in a while, maybe you wouldn't be so weak," Norm says. "I mean, veggies can only take you so far.

Abby rolls her eyes.

Darlene is looking at me, ignoring all of this banter. "Jack, you don't look all right," she says. "Really."

"I'll be okay once I get some sleep," I say.

I, and the rest of the gang, were lucky to not catch the virus that killed most of the world, but we're never lucky enough to catch a full eight-hours. That kind of shit catches up to a guy, no joke.

"Then let's go," Norm says.

5

THE WILTED CROPS WATCH US AS WE WALK UP THE LONG, winding gravel driveway — or at least it seems like it. I can't complain. I'd much rather deal with dead crops than dead people.

Norm leads the way, the baseball bat in hand, but his Magnum not far off. One of the rules I've brought forth from my old zombie book (Sitting on dusty, abandoned shelves at a local bookstore near you!) is never shoot a zombie if you can bash its head in. They are attracted to sound. This is something I learned the hard way back in Woodhaven when I was still trying to get a feel for these creatures, still testing the waters. Like in my book *The Deadslayer,* this proved to be true, among other things: zombies craving human flesh, can only kill them by severing the brain, the putrid stink of rotting bodies, and much, much more.

Norm goes up the stairs first. I am right behind him. Any other time, I'd be there neck in neck with my older brother, but he has the gun while Abby has the other, and I'm pretty beat.

I glance over my shoulder at Darlene. Her fingers are up to her mouth, her teeth working on the nails she once cared so much about. I smile at her, letting her know it's going to be okay.

The front door isn't locked, but it's cracked. This is a good sign. If it was locked, whatever dead things inside of it would still be here.

Norm pushes it open the rest of the way, eases it really. The hinges squeak. I'm not hit with the smell of rotting carcasses. Thank God for small favors, right? But I am hit with the smell of someone else's house. You know what I'm talking about. The smell of home cooked meals and cheap candles from Bath & Body Works, and maybe even cigarette smoke and dog piss. A smell that hits you full-force once you enter, but then disappears about five minutes later only to resurface when you're back in the comfort of your own house, peeling your clothes off while the shower is running, and you're thinking, *How the hell did I stomach that stench for so damn long?*

It's that kind of smell, and in this farm house it's the smell of decaying potatoes, old manure, and maybe rotten eggs and other foods leaking out from behind the closed doors of a refrigerator long since defunct.

These are not pleasant smells, either, but I inhale deeply. It's so much better than dead bodies.

"I think it's clear," Norm says.

I lean back to Abby and Darlene, give them a nod, letting them know they can come in. They do and they stay in the foyer area, closing the door to the outside world.

We aren't even inside and he thinks it's clear, that's how good we've gotten at this. We are human after all. Humans adapt. I swear my sense of smell is heightened, I can see better in the dark, and I'm almost impervious to fear — *almost.* That's cool and all, but I'd be lying if I said I didn't miss the old way of life. Staying up in an air conditioned house, writing, watching TV shows and movies that were once regarded as fiction but have since become the real world, eating whatever I like at whatever time I wanted it (Craving cheeseburgers? McDonald's is open twenty-four hours and it's just down the road). What I miss most of all is the docility. How people weren't always so high strung all the time. You could walk around (at least around my neighborhood in Chicago) without having to worry about people robbing you for your car, your food, your weapons, or your women.

I miss not being a killer. I miss my mother, too, and it's not that if she was still alive I would go see her; it's just that it was nice knowing she was still here, and I could talk to her whenever I wanted to, even if that was only on birthdays and Christmas.

We walk inside, past the little foyer area where the mud caked on the boots next to the door has turned into piles of dust. There's a coat rack with light jackets, workman's gloves, a John Deere hat, then we are in a hallway. There is a washing machine with a load of moldy, mildewy clothes still inside of it. Pictures of Christ on the walls, behind these pictures, a striped wallpaper of earthy colors: brown, a red clay, land-green. Norm takes the left, I take the right.

The right is a family room. The left is the kitchen. There's more though, this place is huge. Apparently farmers make bank and I definitely pursued the wrong career by going into writing. Doesn't matter anymore, though.

Darlene trails behind me, grabs my hand. We walk together in this strange house, both of us on edge, our eyes narrowed, looking for any sudden movement, our breathing low so we can hear every creak and groan.

Inside of the family room is one of those wrap around couches. It stretches wall to wall. There's a folded blanket over the arm. Pillows in the corners, picture-perfect, like a display couch. A film of dust covers the blank screen of the television. It's got to be around fifty inches, and it will most likely never be watched again. There's a large cobblestone fireplace that takes up the bulk of the right side of the room, the type of fireplace I always wanted when I was younger. On the mantle is a framed picture.

They are this house's last owners. God knows where they are now. I take one off of the mantle, the smallest one. The frame is golden and jagged. This was a happy family. An older man in a button-up shirt and black slacks, the shirt tucked in, with his arm around a woman in her mid-fifties wearing a flowery dress, both with deep suntans, both looking like they'd never worn formal wear in their entire lives. Next to them, locked at the elbows is a pair of twins, young men in their caps and gowns, perfect white teeth on their faces. A billowing water fountain is behind them in the shape of an open rose bud. The little stenciled date in the corner of the picture says FSU 2013. They graduated from Florida State. This moment, frozen in time, is now in my hand, and I feel like crying.

Maybe they're still happy. Maybe they're out there somewhere, doing what Darlene, Abby, Norm, and I are doing. Surviving.

Darlene's hand is on my back. I feel the slight tremors going through her body as if she's holding in sobs.

I turn to her. "It's okay," I say. "It's okay."

I know it's not.

"They sat here," she says. "They sat right in here and laughed, watched TV, opened presents on Christmas."

"I know, Darlene, but they're in a better place, now," I say.

"How do you know they've gone to a better place?" Her eyes are glistening.

I don't answer. She just hugs me, wraps her arms tight around my neck. Her hair no longer smells like cherries, but that's okay. I am home when I am with her, that's all that matters.

"Uh, you guys want some privacy?" Norm says from the doorway. Abby is right behind him, a smirk on her face.

There's no longer any privacy among us, and even if me and Darlene went upstairs to an empty room, locked the door, and got our privacy, I wouldn't like it. It's too quiet in here. No hum of air conditioning, no sounds of cars going down the road. Norm and Abby would hear everything. Besides, this is not our house. It belongs to the family forever frozen in happiness in my hand. I don't care if they never come back to claim it. It's just not right.

"No, it's okay," I say. I go to the couch, sit down. The cushions are rigid as if no one has ever sat where I sat, but a smell of stale body odor and old manure wheezes out. "Everything clear?"

"Yeah," Norm says. "Downstairs is good. Abby checked upstairs. Basement is locked, but I'm not about to break the door down to find out what's down there. This place isn't our home, it's just a temporary haven, and it's as empty as a graveyard, far as I'm concerned." He smiles at me.

That's one of our inside jokes. *As empty as a graveyard.* It means that all the dead have risen and nowadays people don't die. Therefore, no more graveyards. The whole world is one.

"Were there any..." I trail off.

Norm shakes his head.

Abby does the same. "Nothing," she says.

I want to ask if she found the family from the pictures, but I don't for Darlene's sake. When the plague swept the nation, then the world, it did so with brutal force. The government didn't do what you'd expect, what they do in every zombie movie and book from here to China. They didn't declare a quarantine because it was too late. They didn't develop a vaccine as quickly as possible because they couldn't. By the time they realized how far this disease spread, it was everywhere. So they pretty much said, *'Hey, well I guess we're all fucked. So you're on your own!'*

Anyway, when the news broke, a lot of people — families like the family who owned this house — took to solving the crisis themselves. Some of them fought, and maybe ended up in places like Eden, but some of them put the barrel of a shotgun in their mouths.

Sad but true.

"Well, what do we do now?" Abby says.

"We rest," Norm says. "Until we're ready to get back

on the road again. I'll do some scouting. See if they left anything of use."

"Let me help," I say.

Norm shakes his head. "No, little brother. You need to rest the most."

"I can rest when we get to Eden." The images of orange groves and smiling people from my dreams come to me.

"If you don't rest now, you'll never get to Eden," Norm says.

Also sad and also true.

6

TODAY, FOR THE FIRST TIME IN A LONG TIME, DARLENE and I will get to sleep by ourselves in an actual bed, mattress and all. No Norm. No Abby. No cramped and uncomfortable folded-down backseats of Norm's long lost Jeep.

We all get our own rooms, our own beds. These rooms are not what I expect. They seem lived-in. Ruffled blankets. Mattresses with the previous owner's body imprinted in the sheets. I go into the bathroom of the one Darlene and I take. I think it might've belonged to one of the farmer's twin sons because of the *Star Wars* posters on the walls. A dead video game console connected to the equally dead television. But in the bathroom my heart stops. Crest toothpaste, the blue kind with the thin squares of breath-freshening mint strips dispersed throughout, sits on the lip of the sink, its cap open. A toothbrush sits next to it. My heart stops for two reasons. The first is that maybe whoever was here before us is still here, only out and about on a supply run, and the second is that maybe this house has running water, maybe it comes through the pipes from a well somewhere nearby. God, I'd kill for a hot shower.

Both of these reasons are proven wrong as I rub my finger across the toothpaste. It is dry, mummified. The head of the toothbrush is dryer than this, and the faucet only sputters and chokes when I turn the knob.

Darlene pops her head around the door frame, her blonde hair no longer bouncy and voluminous, but now clinging to her scalp and face in clumps. "Everything okay?" she asks.

I nod.

But she knows. The rest of her body, noticeably thinner, yet still gorgeous enters the view. "No, it's not, Jack. You look like you saw a ghost."

We've all seen ghosts.

Darlene stares at me expecting an answer so I have to give her one. I say the first thing that pops into my head. "No. No ghost."

She nods as if she knows exactly what I'm talking about, and in a sense, she does. The last six months have been harder on her than the rest of us. She — unlike Norm, Abby, and me — had stakes in the old world. She had family and friends. Now they're gone.

Sometimes, I hear her sniffling in the night. Sometimes I hear her calling out for her mother or her sister in her sleep. It hurts me more than anything else to see her upset and broken. Sometimes, I don't know what to do. I hold her and kiss her, but those gestures can only go so far.

We leave the bathroom and head for the bed. The first angry grumbles from the storm begin to make themselves heard.

I fell asleep at three in the afternoon, and I dream of Eden. Of walls and food and safety. Of seeing whoever wrote the sign on the roof we saw with a smile on their face. It's a semblance of the old world, and it's the reason I wake up. I have to get there for my family, for Darlene and Abby and Norm.

But for some reason, I wake up sweaty and scared.

Outside, it is raining. The storm has passed. I have slept through the worst of it. Distant rumbles of thunder can be heard, streaks of lightning can be seen, but other than that, the field of dead crops and the surrounding woods are quiet and silent. I wake feeling rested, ready to take on the whole dead world by myself.

Darlene is gone next to me, twitching softly every minute or so as I sit there looking out the window. I hear her murmur a name, but it's impossible to tell who it belongs to. I lean over and kiss her on her sweaty cheek. I hope she is having pleasant dreams. I hope she is escaping this fucked-up world, if only just for a minute.

I get up, head downstairs to use the restroom. The plumbing doesn't work in the house as I discovered earlier, but I've not stooped low enough to take a piss in a waterless toilet bowl in a house that's not mine. Plus the storm has settled down enough for me to see the surrounding fields. No fog. No yellow eyes.

The air outside is fresh, that smell of wet soil and leaves. No rotting corpses drifting this way today. I reckon it's around eleven at night. I've gotten my doctor recommended eight hours, but I also reckon I'll sleep for eight more hours, barring a major setback.

I do my business off the back porch where I can see the tops of trees swaying in the faint moonlight breaking through the dark storm clouds. It's calm out here. It's fresh. You can almost forget about all the bullshit you've been through over the past few months. All the hate. All the death. All the darkness. For this moment, the world is how it used to be. I stand, watching the leaves, hearing them rustle for what seems like only a short time.

"You all right?" Norm says from behind me.

I hear his voice through a wave of longing. I am at the bottom of the pool of my pleasant memories, drowning, and Norm is standing on the edge, shouting for me to grab his hand.

"Huh?" I say, shaking my head.

"You've been out here for ten minutes, man," he says. "Can't sleep?"

"I slept like a rock," I say.

"I was getting worried," Norm says. "You were a statue."

The sky has begun to take on a purplish, bruising color. The world is hurt. This disease has pummeled it, and no longer do we see the blackness. Now, we see its wounds.

"I was just thinking," I say, looking at the sky beyond the trees.

"Yeah, about what?"

I don't answer. Norm is not the same guy I remember from my childhood. He doesn't boss me around or hit me or bully me. He's grown up. Still, I don't dare spill my feelings to him. It would not be manly. It would be the kind of stuff only *'pussies'* talk about. I don't exactly know why I feel like this. We've both grown in ten years, and I like who we've become. Maybe I'm afraid if I say what's on my mind, I'll break that fragile illusion.

"Jacky," he says, waving his hand in front of my face. Without much light, I barely see it, just the gleam of the moon in his eyes.

"I...was just thinking about what our next move is," I say.

A lie.

"Easy," Norm says. He walks up next to me, places

his hands on the railing of the back porch. "We get to Eden."

"It's not that easy anymore," I say. "It's so bad out there, and it gets worse every passing minute. There's times when I don't think we're going to make it to the next town."

He claps me on the back. "But we do, little brother! Don't we? Besides, we only need to make it to one more town and then we're *home*."

He says home like we've been on an extended vacation, not like we are showing up to some fabled safe haven with our hands out expecting food, water, and shelter. We don't even know where Eden is for sure. It's like the lost city of Atlantis in this zombie-ravaged world. We just know it's past Sharon or so we *hope.*

"Together, Jack, we can do whatever the fuck we want. Screw these deadheads man. Screw them right up their rotten assholes."

I smile, let out a small chuckle. Norm has always had a way with words. I'm glad the military didn't beat that out of him.

He smiles back.

"Think the girls are going to be okay?" I ask.

Norm nods. "Yeah, they'll come around. Abby already has. Darlene will, too. It might take some close call or tragedy — God forbid — to snap her out of the world we used to live in, but she'll come around."

"I hope so," I say, knowing my hope is misplaced. If a zombie apocalypse can't wake her up, then I don't know what can. There's mourning, that's okay. Things happen and you get upset about them, but you keep moving on, and so far, Darlene has shown me she's not moving at all, not even trying to move on.

"Don't worry, little bro," he says, then turns to look at the dark forest.

I can't help but think of the creatures lurking around out there, watching us with golden eyes. It brings goosebumps up all over my flesh. Zombies are one thing in the Florida daylight, but at night, they are a different beast. At night, all your courage disappears, your past zombie slaying experience with it.

I turn away from the forest, leaning my back up against the railing.

There's a drawn out silence. A calm, perhaps. I turn to Norm, already feeling the words bubbling from my lips, already mentally preparing myself for a right-handed slug in the chin or a sucker punch to the gut.

"Why did you leave?" I ask.

He arches an eyebrow. "What are you talking about? I never left. God knows I wanted to after the shit we saw in Woodhaven and Indianapolis."

I shake my head. "That's not what I'm talking about," I say. Now, I can't help myself. The words just come pouring out. Over a decade of questions sit inside of my head, piling on top of each other. I've been quiet for the six months we've been together, but now the dam bursts. "I'm talking about me and Mother. Why did you leave us? Why did you leave *me?*"

Norm snorts, rolls his eyes. "Oh please, Jack, you didn't like me. I was a shit brother."

"No, I didn't like you. I *loved* you. You're family. I'd love you no matter what. But you didn't have to leave. You didn't even say goodbye! You just left. Do you remember? Do you remember, Norm?"

He recoils, the overconfidence usually lighting his eyes up dimming.

"Do you realize what you did to Mother, to our little family unit? Dad left us, you left us, then I left Mother."

"I had to, Jacky. You don't understand."

I don't know whether to be sad or angry or plain-fucking-ecstatic that I'm finally broaching this subject. So I must look like a madman. My fists clenched, ready for a fight, a misplaced smile on my face, tears threatening to spill down my cheeks.

"Make me understand," I say. "Make me!" My voice is loud. If there are any zombies in the woods looking for their next meal, I pretty much give them an open invitation.

"I can't," he says.

"Was it Mom? Was it me? Was it that fucking town?" I say, my voice shaking. It's now I realize I'm inches away from Norm's face. He is taller than me, not by much, but it's as if I'm towering over him, looking down at a scared, sheltered, seventeen-year-old version of himself.

"Jack, I can't...it's too — "

"What? Embarrassing? Painful? Stressful? Open your eyes, Norm, this whole world is all of those things and more."

Norm takes a deep breath and looks away from me to the wet wood of the back deck. I'm beginning to feel like a grade-A asshole. Like a bully. Freddy and Pat Huber come to mind. Norm over a decade ago. I'm not that. I strive to not be that.

My arm reaches out to Norm, but he turns his back on me. "Fine," he says. "You really want to know? You want to know my deepest, darkest secret? The reason I had to get away from Mom and you—from Woodhaven?"

"Norm, I — " I start to say, but he cuts me off.

"You remember Tim Lancaster?" he asks me. The overconfidence usually in his eyes is not back, but is replaced with a fire instead. The same fire that fills his eyes before a kill.

Tim Lancaster, I think. That's a blast from the past if I've ever heard one, but it's a name that brings up a wave of emotions. He was Norm's best friend for as long as I remember. They were inseparable in middle school. Late-night Nintendo, guzzling Mountain Dew and shoveling pizza, sleeping over all weekend at each other's houses type of buddies. Then when they got to high school and people started to sort off into different social factions — the nerds, the geeks, the jocks, the drama queens — like I experienced first-hand a year after Norm left us, Tim and my older brother remained as inseparable as they always had been. I remember Tim coming over the day after Norm had gone, long before the first letter from basic training in Fort Benning arrived. He asked why Norm wasn't answering his calls, why he stood him up for basketball at Red's Park. I said I thought you knew. Knew what? That Norm left. I handed him the scrap of paper he left on the kitchen table, the paper that mentioned nothing of Tim Lancaster. Tim nodded as if he understood all of this, then he started crying. I was thirteen. I wouldn't cry, though I wanted to. I was stuck in that weird limbo between childhood and manhood. Too afraid to show my emotions. That was the last time I saw Tim Lancaster. He moved that summer to stay with his grandparents in Lansing, Michigan. Last I heard, he had gone on to an art school in New York. I hope that worked out for him. I hope he had a decent life before all of *this* happened.

"Yes, I remember," I say. My voice is weak. A million scenarios are playing out in my head. Maybe Norm and Tim killed someone. I know in high school they'd picked up another hobby — drinking — and Tim had a pretty nifty, hand-me-down, shit-brown

Mercury they cruised around in. Maybe they were drunk driving, struck a homeless man, buried him, and Norm's guilt and fear caused him to run. Maybe —

"I was in love with him," Norm says.

This is a very confusing slap to the face. Love?

"Like friends?" I say.

Norm shakes his head. He looks ashamed, now. There's a chair a few steps behind him, rain pooled in the cushion. He falls onto it, crumpling his normally rigid, soldier-like stature into a ball, and sending small sprays of water in every direction. "No, I was in love with him. Love, Jack. Love like you and Darlene's love."

"Norm...you're gay?" I feel my brain practically explode. My macho older brother...gay. Who would've thought?

"Yeah. Whoop-dee-freaking-doo."

"I-I'm not judging. I'm just — "

"Surprised? Yeah, I bet. There, are you happy?"

I hate to shake my head, but I do. "What does that have to do with you leaving?"

Norm sits up, his elbows on his thighs, face in his hands. He pinches the bridge of his nose as if whatever he's about to tell me is so obvious that I must have developed a mental handicap after he left.

"You know Mom — Mother, " he corrects himself. "She would shove the closest sharp object in her ears if you said the word 'Penis' around her. Don't you remember that one Thanksgiving at Grandma and

Grandpa Dean's house when we were all going around saying what we were thankful for, and I got you to say you were thankful for big tits?"

"Yeah, you told me they called grandparents big tits in France and everyone would be impressed with me knowing a second language. Mother just about passed out, then she whooped my ass out in the garage, hitting me and clicking the automatic door opener over and over again to drown out the sounds of my screams. I was only six, dude!"

Norm is beside himself laughing. If the sun was out, I think I'd see tears streaming from his face. I can't help but smile with him.

"Exactly," he says. "She was uppity. I wanted to tell her for the longest time how I felt about men, but I had no one to talk to. No one would understand. And then one Saturday when she was working a double at Gerry's Diner — or so I thought — she caught me and Tim with our pants around our ankles."

I try not to picture this.

"She didn't react how I'd expected," he continues. "Hell, if I caught my son doing *that* with another fella, I'd probably cut his balls off." He rubs his eyes with the heels of his hands as if trying to rub the image of our mother's silent fury from his retinas.

I inch forward. "Well," I say, "what did she do?"

"She didn't do anything. Her jaw didn't drop to the floor, her eyes didn't catch fire and melt from their sockets, she didn't scream. She kind of just stood there shaking her head, giving us that look — you know the look I'm talking about — while me and Tim tried to cover ourselves up.

Then for the next couple weeks, *months*, she wouldn't talk to me. She wouldn't hear my apologies. I was lost, Jack. I didn't know what I was supposed to do, I just knew I had to get the fuck out of there and away from her."

I feel a spark of anger, remembering how my mother was when Norm left. But I can't blame Norm. There were times when I wanted to leave, too. Ultimately, I did.

Norm stands up now. He stands like his normal self. Rigid. Poised. "I know," he says. "I know I fucked up. I was young and stupid. Scared. Impressionable. One of those Army recruiters stopped me at the mall not long after Mother caught us. I'd just graduated high school — barely, I mean by the skin of my teeth, Jack — and I knew I wasn't going to college. I wasn't like you, man. I don't have a way with words. I ain't a math geek. The world map to me is the USA, Mexicans, Blacks, sissy Europeans, and Terrorists. I can't tell you where Iraq is or where the Queen of England sits on her throne. I'm dumb, and the Army had a lot of great benefits for a dummy like me. I met some great people, went to some great places, but I also did some bad shit. Shit I'm never going to live down. If I could go back in time, I would, Jacky, believe me."

I don't know whether to feel angry or sorry for my older brother. So I don't speak anymore. It doesn't bother me that Norm is gay; it just bothers me that he left us out to dry. I look him square in the eyes, and I can tell he's expecting me to punch him in the jaw. Maybe he'd accept that punch graciously, I don't know, but I have no urge to do it.

Instead, I hug him, and he hugs me back.

"You gonna be okay to stand watch?" I ask.

"Yeah," he says. "Abby will take over pretty soon."

"Good," I say.

Norm and I split up. He must linger on the back deck for a while because I don't hear him come back inside. I go upstairs.

Darlene turns her head to me, says in a sleepy voice: "Everything okay? I heard shouting."

"Yeah, darling, it's okay, go back to sleep."

She does.

I stare up at the ceiling, thinking of Tim Lancaster, of my mother, and of my brother. Sleep comes easier once Darlene's steady breathing fills the quiet. She no longer murmurs. I fall asleep feeling better than I ever have because I know Norm and I have cleared the air. There are no more secrets. It's a good feeling.

7

When I wake up, Norm isn't on the back deck anymore. It is early morning, sunlight streams in through the blinds. Dust floats around the entire room, like small snowflakes in the middle of a hot, Florida summer.

Darlene is gone. I hear footsteps downstairs, laughter. Dishes clank off on another. The girls are fixing a breakfast, out of what, I have no idea. If I had to guess, I'd say it was stale Doritos and flat Coca-Cola. Gone are the days of fresh bacon and eggs and orange juice. None of these sounds are what caused me to wake up. What did it was the sound coming above me.

Clunky footsteps and out of tune whistling.

My heart drops to my stomach for a second, thinking the real owner of this farmhouse has come back, then I hear Norm's gruff voice. "Fuck me," he says.

I cross over to the window, open it. It squeals slightly but other than that opens just fine. Norm is sitting near the red chimney, his pants covered in powdery rust, legs almost hanging off the roof.

"What are you doing?" I say.

He smiles goofily at me. His eyes are red. I doubt he got much sleep last night. "I'm just enjoying the sunshine, little brother," he says, then hiccups.

"Who's on watch?" I ask, feeling that anger bubbling inside of me again.

There's an empty bottle leaning against the bricks next to him. I point to it.

"I am," he says.

"Where did you get that?" I ask, pointing to the bottle.

He shakes his head. "Which one of you said that?" His finger points at me, but slowly moves back and forth as if he is seeing double.

"The booze, Norm, where did you get the booze?"

He looks to the empty bottle, picks it up, closes one eye and peers into it. Then he's patting it on the bottom, trying to get the last drop out with no such luck.

"Found it," he says. "Found a whole bunch of them in the shed. Food, too. But booze first. *Glug, glug, glug.*" He squints his eyes, then puts a hand on his brow to shield the sunlight. He's already deeply tanned, but I can see his skin starting to blister.

"Don't move, Norm. I'm gonna get you off of there before you fall and break your neck."

He shoots up, one foot slipping down the sloped roof. He stumbles, almost falls, and has to grab the chimney to steady himself. "Wait! We're saved! Look! Look! It's a car. We're saved, Jacky!"

I lean out the window, hoping my brother is just having some kind of drunk hallucination.

But Norm is not wrong. A car has just turned off the distant road and into the dirt driveway that leads to the farmhouse. Clouds of dust billow around the back tires. It's a car I wouldn't expect a farmer to own. A souped-up Dodge Challenger as black as the tar that pours out of the zombie's mouths.

Norm jumps up and down, waving his arms. I lean out of the window and try to grab him, but he's too far. "We're over here!" Norm shouts. "Over here!"

"Everything okay?" Darlene says from the first floor. "We got food, Jack. Norm found a freezer running on a generator. Eggs and steak. Fresh. You hungry, Jack?"

I don't answer, and I hear her coming up the wooden steps. When she sees me almost fully out the window and Norm parading around on a sloped roof, she screams. Her hand grabs at the elastic waistband of my underwear. The stitches stretch as my body leans forward. I may have survived a similar fall off a roof half a year ago, but I had Pat Huber and bushes to soften the blow. There's nothing but hard ground to cushion this one.

The Dodge's engine revs.

Another hand grips me around the shoulders, dainty but strong. It's Abby, and with her help, I land on the bedroom's thin carpet.

"We have to go," I say. "We have to get out of here. There's a car. They saw us. Norm is drunk and he's gonna get us killed."

"Wait, hold on, what?" Abby asks. "Slow down."

A gun goes off. The bullet strikes the chimney in an explosion of red dust.

Norm wavers, his hand still around the brick, and brings his own gun out with his other hand. He pulls the Magnum's trigger.

I hear the tires squeal, the spray of rocks dinging the house below.

"Yeah, that's right!" Norm shouts. "You better run!"

But they don't.

I look out the window in time to see another bullet slam into the chimney. Too close. Norm loses his balance, bellowing, and starts sliding down the shingles.

"Norm!" I shout, and I lunge for the window again.

8

Norm's head is bleeding, his eyes are wide. His voice no longer has that drunken, syrupy sound to it. But somehow, he hangs on to the gutter running along the edge of the roof. "Help me! Help!"

"I'm coming!" I shout.

I go out the window, this time more carefully. The shingles are slippery, but my bare feet grip them as well as they can. I jump the gap between this wing of the house and the wing Norm hangs from, and I land with a jarring *thunk*.

Norm whimpers. The gutters creak and groan, threatening to collapse, sending him splattering on the concrete.

I wrap my arms around the chimney and lay on my stomach, all while outstretching my underwear clad legs.

Another gunshot *thwaps*, and before the shot's muted echo leaves my head, I'm showered in a storm of brick-dust. This was probably not the brightest idea, but I can't let my brother die.

Norm grips my ankle, but his hands are sweaty. I feel them slipping. The Dodge has pulled up to the side of the farmhouse, parked horizontally. I see gray hair poking out from the open driver's side door. I see the gun raise, and another shot goes off, silent. It misses me and does the same as the two before it. This bullet strikes dangerously close to my fingers. I can feel the heat radiating from the hole.

Norm's Magnum has long since fallen off and I'm too busy hanging on for dear life to shoot a gun right now.

"Don't shoot!" I yell. "We aren't your enemy!" As if I really know that.

From the corner of my eye, I see Abby hang out the window. For a split second, I think she's going to start shooting, but she doesn't. She has a pillowcase in hand and she's waving it like a surrender flag. It's not white. It's yellow. It'll have to do.

I think the guy gets the hint because the shots stop.

Norm crawls up my leg, his fingers digging into my flesh, then pulling on my underwear. My bare ass is visible to God and everyone else, but Norm makes it up the roof.

His eyes are clear, his breathing ragged. Yeah,

plummeting to your death will sober you up real quick.

"Who are you?" the man from the Dodge shouts. From up here, I can see his mane of silver hair shining in the Florida sunlight. "What the hell are you doing in my house?" He leans into the car and says something in a quiet voice. I catch the last bit of what is said. "Go! Go!" The windows are tinted and I can't seem to see who it is, but someone gets out, and rushes around the front of the house.

I scramble to the window, ready to jump, ready to put myself between Darlene and Abby, to protect my family.

"I want whoever is in the house to come out. No weapons. No tricks. No funny business. I mean it! I got my sights set on both of your friends's heads, and I won't hesitate to repaint my roof with their blood. Understood?" the silver-haired man says.

Abby and I catch eyes. I nod to her. It pains me to not put up a fight, but I've already done one stupid thing today, and the day is pretty young. I don't need any more blood on my hands.

Darlene's sunburnt face seems to drain of all color. "I know you're scared," I say to Darlene, "but it will be okay. I promise."

She smiles with trembling lips.

I almost believe myself.

9

Abby and Darlene stand in front of the Dodge with their hands up. Norm is beside me, his face sweaty, his skin waxy. I think he might vomit.

Abby talks in a low voice, explaining our situation.

The older man with the gray hair doesn't take his sights off of me. His beard is longer than the hair on his head, and a gaunt man stands next to him, nodding as Abby talks. This man's hair is long, a jet black, and his beard is scraggly but not as long as the older man's. He also has a gun, but it's in his hand, resting on the side of his thigh.

The older man nods to the younger one, and the younger one disappears. Abby turns to me and gives me a thumbs up. What's that supposed to mean? They won't kill us as gruesomely as we think? They'll let us go?

Norm leans over the roof, his hands covering his mouth, but not fast enough. Puke spews from between his fingers, splattering me. It's not a thumbs up moment at all.

"Oh, man," he says, "I feel so much better."

About two minutes later, I'm crawling down a ladder with Norm's puke drying on my t-shirt. He's on the ground. Abby practically holds him up.

"That all of you?" the older man says, the gun still trained on me.

I am annoyed and I am scared. The zombie apocalypse not only brings out the worst in corpses, but also people. These guys could be cannibals, rapists, murderers. How am I supposed to know? And we just succumb to them without so much as a fight.

"Yeah, that's all," Darlene says. "We are telling the truth."

"We'll see about that," the old man says.

He circles behind us.

"Want me to unload, Pa?" the younger man asks.

My blood freezes. Unload? What is this, a firing squad?

"No, Bri, not in front of them. Not until I seen what they've been up to inside."

"All right, Pa, but I don't think we have much to worry about. That one just vomited off the roof. Dummies, if you ask me. Surprised they made it this long."

I'm not bothered. He is right, Norm was stupid, and in about three hours when the booze headache hits him square in the noggin, he'll be *really* sorry.

We walk up through the front door.

The old man sniffs deeply. "Wow, y'all found my steak and eggs, I see." He spins around, the harsh light streaking in through the thin curtains shading the windows cause him to look crazy. A man on his last thread of sanity. Can I blame him? We did break into his house after all.

"In the kitchen," the old man says.

We follow him, the younger man behind us.

"Have a seat," he says. "I'd like to know who has been staying in my place. Whether I should punish them or not." Yeah, I'd like to see him try. Then he turns to the younger man. "Wouldn't you, Brian?"

Brian nods.

The older man pulls out a chair and sits down. His weapon is something James Bond would use, a sleek, black pistol with a silencer on the end. He aims it at the four of us.

"What's your names? I'm Tony. Tony Richards," he says. "Please have a seat."

My eyes drift back to the gun he holds on us. Not the first time I've had one pointed at me, but I make it seem like it is. "It'd be a lot easier to talk if I wasn't fearing for my life," I say.

Tony looks down at the pistol as if he forgot it was

there. He chuckles. "This old thing? It's just precautionary. You understand, I'm sure."

"You don't have to worry about us," I say.

I expect Norm to say something stupid here. His macho side is apt to show up during times where our backs are *literally* up against the wall. I get none of that. Instead he leans forward, his head in his hands, and mumbles something about needing an aspirin.

"I already told him that," Abby says as if I could hear what the hell they were talking about while I was dangling, puke-covered, from this man's roof.

"And that's exactly what one of Spike's men would say to cover his ass," Tony says.

I lean forward. Flakes of Norm's vomit fall from my shirt onto this guy's dinner table. I catch it falling out of the corner of my eye, and suddenly the aroma of steak and eggs doesn't seem so enticing. "Listen, Tony Richards, I don't know who Spike is, but you do realize with your logic, you are pretty much saying you're going to kill us."

Tony ponders this a moment, scrunching his forehead up. I know his type. Like this before the world went to shit, camouflage hunting vests, fake testicles dangling from the back bumper of the truck which is too big for him to get in and out of comfortably, a wad of chew packed tight in between rotting teeth and cheek. This is the type of guy you'd expect to survive the zombie apocalypse. Redneck. Second Amendment defender. Don't get me wrong, I have nothing against these types of people. I'm pretty open-minded, and the end of the world has made that even more true (I mean, I've considered eating bugs, man), but I do have something against them when they're pointing a gun at my family.

"I guess you're right," Tony says. He smiles. It's a pained smile. A moment of realization hits me. Tony Richards is older and covered in stress-wrinkles and a long, gray beard, but he is a man whose face a smile does not belong. He is the man in the picture with his wife and twin sons. The picture on the mantle. This is not how I thought I'd meet him. Hell, I never thought I'd actually meet him.

"Is that your son?" I ask. "Is that your twin boy?"

The smile vanishes. The gun is now in my face, inches away. "How would you know that? I don't know you. I've never met you. You'd only know that if you was working for Spike."

"No," I say. "I saw the picture."

Darlene scoots a little closer to me. She is shaking, visibly shaking. Times like these, I'd put my arm around her and calm her down, but I can't.

"What the hell do you want from us?" I say. "If you're going to kill us, don't draw it out. Just fucking do it." I puff out my chest, looking more like a chicken than a brave man. This is usually the point Norm intervenes with his macho side.

I'm doing my best.

"To the point," Tony says, nodding. "I like that." He lowers his pistol. "I'll get to the point, too, then, I guess. Seeing as y'all's on my property, I don't think what I plan to do with you is any of your gosh darned business."

Brian nods and folds his arms. For the moment, I see the resemblance. I see the similarity from the photo sitting on the mantle in Tony Richards's living room. He doesn't look as young anymore. He looks like he's seen some shit, but we all have. The wispy hair on his face hides most of the recognizable features, and he's lost a good ten to fifteen pounds.

Tony turns to look at him. If I ever had a chance to break out of here, it would be now. I would, too, if Norm wasn't half-zonked out of his mind. He's been constantly moaning the entire time we've been at the table. We are outmatched. We are outgunned.

"What you think, son? Should I let them go? Or make them pay?"

Brian nods his head from side to side. "Like I said, they're too dumb to be part of Spike's crew."

"Well, friends, today's your lucky day," Tony says.

"Lucky because I'm stuck in a house with an old redneck, staring down the wrong end of a gun. Yeah, lucky as hell," I say.

Tony smiles the smile that looks so misplaced. Brian does not.

"Lucky because I'm letting you go. All of you," Tony says.

"Why is that?" I ask, narrowing my eyes at him. It's almost too good to be true.

"Shut up, Jack," Darlene says. "Don't question him."

Abby nods, her eyes wide.

Norm doesn't do anything. He's pretty much dead to the world.

"Yeah, Jack," Tony says, grinning. "Don't screw it up, now. Who knows how I'll feel in a minute or two. I might decide I want to punish you for breaking into my house." His look goes from me to the gun. I know he's full of shit. He might have killed before, but he is not a killer. He is a family man. He is a farmer.

But I won't risk it.

I stand up. "Fine, we'll get out of your hair. And we apologize for breaking into your house."

"Lovely home by the way," Darlene says as she follows my lead. "I love what you've done with the place."

Tony smiles, but it's not that uncomfortable, genuine one. It's a fake.

"Yeah, sorry," Abby says.

"Come on, Norm," I say, placing a hand on his shoulder. "Let's go."

He mumbles.

“We’re gonna have to carry him out of here,” Abby says, giving him a shake.

“He’ll make it to Eden,” I say.

And it’s like the air is sucked out of the room.

Brian pulls a gun free from the back of his waistband, points it at us. Tony lifts his off the table, gets up so fast, the chair he was sitting on flips behind him.

“Liars!” Tony shouts.

My heart drops. Abby almost trips over her own feet. Darlene shrieks and puts herself behind me.

“You know about Eden! You fuckin dirty liars!” Brian says. “Y’all said you didn’t. They’re working for him, Pa!”

Tony gets this menacing look on his face and grabs the pistol. “Send Spike my regards.”

10

MAYBE THE OLD ME, THE ONE WHO I THINK DIED IN THE Great Fire of Woodhaven last year, — yeah, that's what I'm calling it now — would shit his pants and let this old geezer boss me around. Let him jam a gun in my face. But that's not me anymore. Norm isn't all there to back me up, so I have to act fast.

I slap the pistol from his hand. It goes flying behind him, the silencer thumps the counter, and lets off a muffled shot into the peeling, striped wallpaper.

Tony's face turns up into a snarl. Seriously, add a bit of blood and make him smell a little worse and you'd think he was one of the zombies.

His son aims at me, but Abby is on him fast as ever. She's grown into quite an athlete since we've been on the road. I'm almost too impressed to punch Tony in the face.

Almost.

I cock back and slug the old man across the jaw. His bones aren't brittle. They must be made of steel because my knuckles explode with white-hot pain.

Still, Tony stumbles over his overturned chair and lands in a heap. An empty dog bowl goes spinning across the linoleum floor, its silver catching rays of sunlight filtering in through the kitchen window.

I reach for the gun.

Darlene screams behind all of the chaos, a dazed and seemingly half-dead Norm in her arms. "Stop! Stop it!"

She senses the blood about to be spilled. She senses the kill in the air.

So do I.

I grab the gun, the cold iron filling my hand, sending buzzes of powerful electricity through my skin.

Tony sees me, and I must look crazy again because he scoots himself across the floor until he hits the dead refrigerator and puts his hands up. "Please, don't please."

A calm washes over the room. I feel all eyes on me, even Norm's. Abby has since subdued the skinny, young man. He's on his knees, his head down, and his shaggy, black hair hanging over his face. His hands are up half-heartedly, but he wants to die. I can see it as much as I can feel it. He wants Abby to end his life, and with the end of his life will come the end of the suffering, the nightmares, the constant looking over your shoulder.

Tony Richards, the old man, he doesn't want to die. He wants to live.

"Stop, Jack. Stop it! This isn't you," Darlene says.

I take a deep, shaky breath. She's right. It's not. But sometimes we have to wear disguises if we want to get what we need.

I aim the gun at the old man's head. My index finger wavers as it brushes the trigger.

"Please," Tony Richards says while his son says nothing. "Please, we can work something out. You all can stay here, if you want."

"With psychopaths who want to kill us?" I say. Even I don't like the way I sound. "I think not."

"You don't understand. Eden? You're from Eden and you don't have feelings. You don't. Spike — I can't go back to him. I escaped once, I'm never going back there," Tony says, babbling. The babbles turn to sobs. He brings a big, callused hand up to his face and wipes away sweat and tears at the same time. "Please, please," he says.

"We aren't from Eden," I say. "We already told you that."

He looks up at me. "You're not?"

"No. We're trying to get there. Geez, man. I'm not your enemy. *We're* not your enemy," I say.

Abby nods.

"Yeah," Norm croaks.

"How did you know about it?" Tony asks. "It-it's supposed to be a secret now."

"Everyone knows!" I shout. "There's signs and clues all over the highway. People talk about it. We're just some of the refugees looking for safe haven."

"Eden is not safe," Tony says. The way he speaks chills me.

I don't know what to say. So many questions come to mind that none of them can come out.

"Jack," Darlene says. "Let's go. Let's leave." Her face is pale, that sunburn drained. I feel the dejected spirit of the group. They don't want to believe Tony's words. Neither do I.

"*Pleaseeee —* " Tony begins again. The rest of his words are choked out by sobs.

I grab the pistol with both hands now, steadying my aim just like Norm taught me. But I do not pull the trigger.

Instead, I hit the magazine release. I let the clip fall to the linoleum and the sound it makes is close to a gunshot. So close, I see Brian shutter to my right and Tony Richards convulse as if I had just shot him. He opens his eyes. Looks around at the drab kitchen then at his son and smiles. "Thank you," he says. "Thank you!"

"I'm not your enemy," I say again.

Abby hasn't lowered her weapon. She's learned that the hard way, too. I know she won't pull the trigger, but what's left of the Richards family doesn't.

Tony's face, which had been growing rosy since he realized I didn't shoot him, begins to drain of all color again.

"You don't want to go to Eden," he says. "I mean it, son."

Then Brian starts laughing. I look over to him. His hair shakes with each deep rumble. "We're so stupid," he says. "So stupid, Dad."

I narrow my eyes at him. "How so?"

He looks up at me. That look is in his eyes, the look that wasn't there before — a man on his last thread of sanity. "We keep our mouths shut about Eden, tell you where to go, how to get there, and then...BOOM! You're dead."

I jump at the sound of his voice.

"Spike sees you coming — believe me, Spike sees everything — and next thing you know, your head is on a pike outside the gates. Then me and my Pa here live out the rest of our days as happy as we can be, never having to worry about you idiots coming back and trying to take what's ours," Brian continues.

"Why should we believe you?" I ask. Eden has to be safe, it just has to.

Brian ignores my comment.

"Too late, Pa! Too late!"

Abby hits him with the pistol. Clobbers him right in the temple, and Brian is a heap of bones on the linoleum.

My eyes bulge at the sight. I have to do a double take to make sure it really happened.

Behind me, Darlene gasps. "Abby," she says as if she's offended.

Abby shrugs. "What? He was creeping me out."

I look at Tony, putting on my fake tough guy voice, the one Norm does so much better. "You're next if you don't tell us more about Eden." It's almost laughable. I'm not cut out for this job.

The voice is shabby, but it seems to do the trick. Tony looks at me with a little more respect than he did before. He knows I'm in control, and that's good enough for me.

"Okay, I'll tell you," he says. "But what's the point? You won't believe me. It was once a place you could go to be safe, but now it's overrun by a madman and his equally crazy followers. You don't want to go there. You don't want to — "

"You're right," I say. "We are going to Eden. You may be lying or you may be telling the truth. One way or the other, I'm finding out for myself. If it's how you say it is, then my group and I will take it back. When we do, we will send a car out here for you, and you and your son can live in peace." Abby and Darlene stare at me. I like to think there is respect written on their faces. Norm is hunched over the back of a chair, his eyes barely open. I try to think more like him and what he would say in a situation like this. "We'll need weapons and a ride if you can spare one," I finally say.

"Don't," Tony says. "Don't go. I have nothing to give you. I cannot help."

"Bullshit," Abby says. "The basement is locked and I'm guessing it's locked for a reason. You got something in there you don't want anyone else to see."

She's right.

Tony is shaking his head. "No," he says. "Don't go down there."

But I'm already moving out of the kitchen toward the small hallway and the basement beyond. "We won't take all of your weapons, just enough to get us there so we can see for ourselves," I shout back, looking over my shoulder.

Tony starts to get up, but Abby is on him with her gun. "Don't move," she says.

11

THE BASEMENT DOOR IS LOCKED, BUT THE LOCK IS NO match for a bullet. I shoot it once, my head turned and my eyes shielded. A metallic whine fills the small corridor.

I open the door. The smell that hits me is a smell of death and decay, a smell I have always associated with basements. Mildew. Dust. Cobwebs.

So I am not surprised.

"Don't go down there!" Tony shouts again.

It's too late.

My right foot already hits the first step. It creaks beneath my weight, and dust and that basement smell wafts up to meet me. It's not the smell that surprises me the most, but the look and feel of the basement. The steps seem to stretch on into the darkness forever. Once I'm on the cobblestone floor, it starts to get weird.

Muted sunlight comes in through a sliver of a window. It's enough for me to see the trail of black blood, and I think that's what the smell that punches me in the nose is.

I try to keep my back to a wall, but this basement is as vast as the house above it. There's hallways and corridors, shelves full of useless trinkets — old oil cans, ancient soda bottles, a mallet, nails, a packet of molding muffins — that stretch to the ceiling where cobwebs hang from a series of interwoven pipes and air ducts. I turn around and the steps seem to have moved to the other side of the room, that's how lost I am already. A pile of old, rotten furniture sits in a corner. Chairs, tables with missing legs, a La-Z-Boy recliner.

I walk on.

The smell grows thicker now. That dead, rotting smell now mingling harshly with the smell of mold and dust and dirt. I almost bring my hand up to cover my nose, but I can't. I have to remain strong. I have to find the weapons. I know they're here.

I turn down a corridor and push a door open with the gun. It creaks loudly, though I can hear my breath above the sound.

As the door opens, I freeze.

These are not guns.

These are bodies. Dead bodies. But not human

bodies...dead zombie bodies. I almost start to scream as I look away, trying to get a hold of myself.

Two bodies strapped to wooden tables.

What in the actual fuck?

I raise the weapon at them. They could be alive — well, you know what I mean — and I don't want to be caught by surprise, attacked because my initial impression is wrong. I try to walk closer to them as quietly as I can, but it's dark and I kick something.

A tin can goes skittering across the floor and bangs into the wall on the other side of the tables.

I hold my breath, watching for any movement.

There is none.

The eyes of these zombies do not glow yellow. They do not make that death rattle deep from their throat. They do not turn their heads and stick out their arms to try to grab me.

They are dead.

I walk closer. The smell of them is like an invisible barrier I don't want to break through.

The little bit of light streaming in through the hallway and into this room shows me who they are — or who they *used* to be. Had I not seen the photograph on the upstairs mantel, these two would just be another couple of zombies. I almost wish they were because I wouldn't feel so sad...so pitiful.

The woman with her long and now brittle blonde hair

stares up at the ceiling with wide eyes. Her lower jaw has been completely ripped off. The dress she wears is new, however, something that looks unworn. She did not die in this dress, I can tell you that. Her face has this sunken-in quality that still somehow tells me she was once beautiful.

The man laying next to her wears an unblemished suit and tie. He is missing an eye. There is a bullet hole in the middle of his forehead caked with dry, crusty blood. He has no facial hair, not like his twin brother upstairs.

This is Brian's twin and his mom, Tony's wife.

I feel like sobbing.

I know what it's like to lose a mother, but I couldn't imagine losing my mother *and* my brother. Screw the guns, they can wait.

I turn out of the room, saying a silent prayer in my head, and go back upstairs.

Norm looks a little better as I walk back into the kitchen. Brian is awake, but I try not to look at him because seeing his dead twin is like seeing him dead. Abby and Darlene watch me eagerly.

"No guns?" Abby asks.

I ignore her and turn to Tony who is still up against the refrigerator. His face is wet, his eyes are shiny.

"You didn't touch them, did you? You didn't touch them?" he says to me.

I shake my head, then squat down to look him in the eyes.

"What the fuck is going on?" Norm says behind me. He almost sounds normal. I ignore him, too.

"I want to help," I say to Tony.

His face transforms from hurt to angry, the color rising in his cheeks. "You can't help! They're already dead! Spike did it to them. It was fucking Spike. You can't help! You can't — "

I put my hand on his arm and squeeze. He looks like he wants to hit me, wants to pounce on me and tear me limb from limb. Rightfully so, I guess. I have invaded his privacy, have stumbled upon something he didn't want anyone to see.

"I want to help, Tony. I will do anything, okay? Then we will be even."

Tony blinks once, tears fall from his eyes.

"Just stay out of our business," Brian says.

I ignore him like I ignore the others.

"Let me help you lay them to rest," I say to Tony.

"I-I can't. I don't want to. I don't want to. I love her. Wendy has been with me forever. And Benny, oh my sweet Benny. I can't, Jack. I just can't."

"I understand, Tony. I do. But you will never move on if you keep them there. And you have to move on. That's what this world is all about. Things happen —

bad things, *terrible* things — but sometimes good things happen, too. If you're stuck in the past, you can't enjoy the future."

"Nothing good is gonna happen. You don't get it, son. You're too young," Tony says. He points to the gun in my hand. "Just put a bullet in my brain. Let me move on that way."

I shake my head.

The tears are streaming down his face. I feel everyone's eyes staring at us.

"I know, I know, it's hard to believe good things can happen now. They might not, and that's true, but we can't say for sure. The only thing I can say for sure is that good things won't happen if you're dead, Tony Richards. You have a son who loves you and respects you. You have to be strong for him."

Tony wipes his eyes with his grimy fingers, takes a deep breath, and nods. "You're right, kid. Damn it, you're right."

"There's a beautiful tree out back. A tree with all its leaves, standing tall and vigilant. It's a perfect place to lay them to rest, Tony. I don't know why I feel that way, but I know if we bury them there, that tree will watch over them for eternity," I say.

Tony lets out a sob mixed with a laugh. I stand up and extend a hand down to him. He takes it, and much to my surprise, he pulls me in for a hug. "Thank you," he says. "Thank you."

Then we part and his son comes over and hugs him.

I look over to Darlene, Abby, and Norm. They are all looking at me with shocked expressions on their faces. I just shrug and head out to the backyard where that big, beautiful tree sways in the light breeze.

I find a shovel near the shed, and I begin to dig.

I dug until the sun started to go down. Not long after my shovel had hit the dirt, Abby, Darlene, and Norm came out to help me. We dug two graves, side by side, right in the tree's shade.

At first, they questioned me, but once I told them about the bodies in the basement, they understood and went right to work. Tony and Brian Richards, like the rest of the world, have begun to lose their sanity. Their loved ones rotted away in the basement of an abandoned farmhouse. If it isn't for us, I believe they would take their own lives. Norm, Darlene, and Abby agree with me.

There is already enough death in this world. If we have any hope of surviving this plague, we must help each other out, we must keep each other alive.

Norm and I helped Tony and Brian wrap Wendy and Ben Richards into sheets. They said their goodbyes. We helped carry them up the steps. They weighed next to nothing and I hardly noticed the smell.

We laid them to rest before the sun went down.

Tony and Ben helped cover them up.

We all cried.

And the remaining members of the Richards family moved on.

As the group gathers up what remaining belongings we left in the farmhouse, Tony and I stand on the front porch. He has two beers in his hand and he gives one to me.

It is cold.

It's been too long since I've had a cold drink. It almost makes me cry.

"Thank you," I say. I down it in three big gulps.

He smiles at me. I notice how much younger he looks. In just the span of a few hours, it seems as if a huge weight had been lifted from Tony Richards's shoulders. "No. Thank you," he says.

He shakes my hand.

Darlene comes out with Norm and Abby behind her. We have all our stuff ready to go. Eden is our next stop. I don't care what stands in our way. We are getting to safety — *true* safety, not a farmhouse without borders, but a safe haven.

Tony looks them up and down, the happiness on his face melting away. "Anyway I can talk you guys out of it?"

I shake my head. "We've come too far. If it's like you say it is, then we will fix it."

"It is, Jack," he says. "And you might not be able to fix it." He pauses, sensing my seriousness, then says, "You may be able to scavenge in Sharon. I don't think Spike and his army have taken much from there yet. Grab all the weapons and medicine you can find. You will need it."

"We'll see," I say.

"Sorry I can't offer you more help, but you understand."

I nod.

Tony did not have weapons to spare aside from a sniper's rifle none of us really knew how to use. Norm claimed he did, but I think that was the booze talking.

"What about the car? You sure you don't want to take it?" Tony asks.

I shake my head. "No, you keep that sweet ride. Walking is good, less noise, less attraction."

"True," he says.

"Well," I say, "it was nice to meet you and your son. May your days be long and prosperous."

Tony smiles. "And yours, too," he says as he begins to shake our hands and say his goodbyes to Darlene, Norm, and Abby.

"Got any more of that booze?" Norm asks.

Tony chuckles.

Abby grabs Norm's arm and drags him away. "You're never drinking again," she says.

I walk off the porch, and give Tony one last wave.

I am leading my group to the small town of Sharon. Beyond that is Eden and what Eden holds in store for us, I do not know. But we will find out.

12

WE WALK IN SILENCE DOWN THE SAME DIRT ROAD WE entered. All we have are two guns between us and a bag of blunt weapons.

All signs of last night's storm have vanished. That's Florida for you. Back in Ohio, a summer thunderstorm would leave the ground sopping wet and the sky a depressing gray for a couple of days. Not the case here. Now, the sun shines and the sky is a clear blue. There's a few clouds which look like puffs of white smoke floating lazily above us. No storm on the horizon.

I think that's a good sign.

The perfect sign to combat the bad ones I saw in the farmhouse. Seeing the two corpses and seeing how it affected Tony — bringing him to a sobbing shell of a man — and Brian hurt me more than I care to admit. In *The Deadslayer*, Johnny Dunbar is a character I tried to write without emotional attachments because that is the perfect character to go around bashing zombie skulls. Turned out, that I couldn't do it in fiction so how could I do it in real life?

Everyone cares about somebody — *something* — and to try to deny that would make us as bad as the zombies themselves.

But it's so much harder trying to survive with the people you care about. Any small thing can ruin it — an impromptu stay at a crazy man's farmhouse, a morning stroll in the fog, a bottle of pure absinthe that fucks your militarily-skilled older brother up beyond recognition.

Abby breaks the silence as she is so apt to do. "What if he is right?" she asks. "Like what if this Spike guy is crazy and Eden is a madhouse."

I look at her, my face a stone slate of seriousness. "Then we'll deal with it. We didn't come all this way and go through all this shit to give up now."

"Damn right," Norm says. "It happens and we deal with it. We all saw it back in Indianapolis. People go crazy when shit hits the fan, it's a basic law of the universe. That's why we can't let it get to us."

I nod.

Norm smirks. "By the way, little brother, that was a good thing you did back there with Tony." He scratches his sunburned neck, a gesture that tells me he's going to give me praise. He's never really comfortable when it comes to that. "Helping them, I mean. If that would've been me who saw a couple of mutilated corpses in the basement of the house I slept in the night before I woulda shot first and asked questions later."

"Thanks," I say. "I just saw how bad they were, how bad they were *getting*. I remembered when I buried Mother, I felt a little better. Not a whole lot, but it took me in the right direction."

Norm nods and claps me on the back. "You're a good man, Jack. Smart, too. Always have been."

I smile at him.

"Sorry, that booze messed me up. Haven't drank like that since Bangkok. Whew. My head is still spinning."

"Don't worry about it," I say.

Abby and Darlene snort, holding back laughter. I look at them and they both are grinning ear-to-ear. "Still," Abby says, "it was funny seeing you like that."

Norm smiles back and gives her a playful punch on the arm. "Can it, Abby," he says, then starts rubbing at his head.

We walk for what seems like half an hour, joking, laughing, and almost forgetting what dangers lie ahead of us. But through all of this, our eyes are sharp, always scanning the surroundings for enemies — human *or* zombie.

The neglect of these roads is clearly visible in the myriad of cracks running through them. The white line in the middle faded. Grass grows from between the deeper splits in the asphalt. No car has driven these streets in a long time. A tree has fallen across the way about thirty feet ahead of us.

We go over it carefully. It reminds me of the tree behind the farmhouse where Wendy and Ben Richards are now buried beneath.

Darlene puts her hand on the small of my back, leans in and kisses me on the cheek. She can always read what's on my mind. Sometimes I hate it — it never lets me win fights...*never* — and sometimes I love it.

Especially now. Maybe everything will be okay.

13

We got to the town about fifteen minutes later. The town is called Sharon, but someone has so cleverly crossed out the name on the sign with bright, red spray paint and wrote DEATH.

A town called Death. I like it. Sounds like it's from a Clint Eastwood western.

As we pass the empty buildings, I notice more signs and symbols spray painted on the bricks and the show windows.

Mostly it's religious babble: JESUS SAVE US, GOD'S WRATH. But one in particular catches my eye. It says, SPIKE IS GOD! SPIKE IS ANGRY! HIDE YOUR HANDS! and it's written across towering church doors. I don't point it out to anyone else, and I hope they don't see it. We don't need to be demoralized. Not now.

It gives me chills. As Darlene turns her head to read the sign, I grab her chin and kiss her. I feel her lips turning to a smile beneath mine.

Farther up ahead, as we break onto the Main Street, the town seems almost untouched. Frozen in time. We walk down the road where the business and bars stand on each side of us like silent watchers. There's cars parked in the diagonal spots in front of them, their windshields dusty and dirty. A large and faded Coca-Cola sign is painted on the side of the tallest building which is only two stories. This was probably the most popular bar in town. The sign on the door reads OPEN.

"Well, take your pick," Norm says to us, motioning to the buildings. "Which one of these do you think has weapons or medicine?"

"None of them," Abby says.

"Probably right," he says. "But it's worth a shot."

"Why don't we split up?" I say.

"I don't think so," Abby says. "Might not be a good idea."

Norm waves his hands around to the empty street. "Look around! Ain't nobody here."

I think of the signs. I think of Tony's warnings.

"Me and Norm and you and Darlene?" I say.

"Fine," Abby says. "Darlene and I will take the shops over there," she points to the side opposite the large Coca-Cola sign and Sharon's most popular saloon, "and you two take over here."

"Sounds good. Ready, little brother?" Norm says.

I watch Abby and Darlene disappear into the dark shops.

"Hey, don't worry about them, little bro," Norm says. "That Abby's got a mouth on her, but she's tough as nails. Darlene'll be all right. Let's go find us something useful."

14

THE FIRST THING I NOTICE IS THE SMELL. THAT ALWAYS seems to be the first thing you notice nowadays. It's not the rotten smell of decaying corpses, but it's a clean smell. A smell of the old world. It's spilled beer long since soaked into the wooden floor and bar top, of stale cigarette smoke, of puke, and bad, drunken decisions.

It's a smell I relish and welcome.

The stools are empty. The televisions are black except for the faint reflections of ourselves and the outside light behind us. I've never been in a bar in the early morning. It's something as a writer I always expected to do. Don't get me wrong, I love the occasional drink, especially when times are tough, and there haven't been tougher times than now. Without Darlene in my life, the occasional drink would've become the occasional no-drink. She keeps me grounded. She makes me better.

"Huh?" Norm says. "End of the world and all, I would've thought more people would've come to drown the pain with some whiskey."

"Maybe you got people wrong," I say.

Really, they were probably too sick to go anywhere.

"No, we're all the same," he says as he walks behind the bar and grabs a dusty bottle of Jack Daniels off the shelf. "We cry when we're upset, piss our pants when we're scared, and drink ourselves to death when none of the other shit works."

"Words of a true genius," I say. "Shakespeare would be proud." I look at the bottle. "You're not really going to drink — "

He downs a large swallow of whiskey as if it were water, not even grimacing, then he shrugs. "You pick up a thing or two in the Army," he says. "Best thing for a hangover is more booze."

"Yeah, I bet," I say.

He holds the bottle out to me. "A little warm, but it's better than nothing."

"No, thanks. I'm gonna check the back."

"All right, little bro. Just holler if you need me. I'm gonna do a little drinking...you know, drown my sorrows." He pours the whiskey on the floor, then points to the ceiling. "That's for Shelly."

Shelly was his Jeep. Ridiculous, I know.

I push through a door that reads EMPLOYEES ONLY.

The kitchen is about as quaint as the bar. There's a microwave, a shelf of snack foods like chips, packaged brownies, and Slim Jim's, some cans of nacho cheese, a refrigerator straight out of the 1970s. The health inspector must not have been due for another year because the counter is spotted with dry bits of chili and cheese, and other crumbs. Beyond the kitchen is a small hallway which leads to an emergency door. There's a window where the Florida morning streams in, lighting my way, but there's no people, dead or otherwise.

I turn around to head out into the bar. The door squeaks, and Norm shushes me. He's squatted down behind a couple of stools, waving me to do the same. I instantly drop. Maybe six months ago, I would've asked questions, but not anymore. When Norm is like this, or anyone in the group for that matter, it means the dead are near.

I see a figure through the dusty bar window. A head bobs between the stenciled letters on the glass which read HOME BASE BAR AND GRILL, except it doesn't move like the dead. It moves like —

The figure turns toward the bar. I hear his voice, quiet, but deep. It carries on the wind. "...saw them go in here, I did. Maybe the book store. I"ll check it, yes I will!" Almost singsongy.

Norm glances at me, that fiery look in his eyes. I nod. He pulls the hammer back on his Magnum, and I get to position with my machete, nimbly walking over the wooden floor, fearing for the creak that will put the nail in my coffin. No such creak comes and I put my back to the wall between window and door. My heartbeat thuds in my chest.

The door opens.

Norm is positioned at the bottom left corner of the bar, his gun raised.

The man comes in through the door with his own gun leading the way. It's a shabby revolver, something a widowed old woman would keep on top of her nightstand in a bad neighborhood. Still, a gun is a gun.

"Drop your weapon," Norm says. "We mean no — "

A gunshot cuts him off. My eyes jam close and when I open them, I see a chunk of the wood floor go up in a spray of splinters. Norm dives out of the way, takes cover behind a few chairs. He's quick, and the table he's nearest falls over, giving him more cover.

I'm not as quick, but I act too.

The person behind the revolver is a large black man, wearing a sweaty wife-beater tank top. His mouth is wide open, eyes closed in pain, as I swing the handle of the machete at his head.

This guy lets out a blood-curdling scream, almost like a whining puppy. It makes me queasy, and when a spray of blood dots my face, I feel even sicker.

The machete handle thunks against the guy's skull. I feel the twanging vibrations of the metal.

The gun drops to the floor, and I'm quick to kick it toward Norm. There's a large gash in the man's scalp. Fresh red dribbles from the wound.

"Why did you d-do that?" the large man yells, blubbering. "Oh my god! My head, you broke-ed my head! Help! Lawd, help me!"

Norm gets out from behind the toppled over table. He picks up the small revolver which pales in comparison to Norm's Magnum, then he looks at the bleeding man on his knees.

We are both stunned to see a man this size crying.

Guilt invades me. "What was I supposed to do? He shot at you!"

Norm shrugs. "I mean, couldn't you have just punched him in the face? You didn't have to rock his bell that hard, champ."

"He's ginormous!" I say.

"No, no, no, please don't hit me a-g-g-g-gain," the guy says.

"You shot at us," I say, this time calmly. "It wasn't personal."

This doesn't seem to register because he screams louder.

I look at the wound. "Not fatal, I say. "It'll be sore for a couple days, but some stitches will do the trick."

"Yeah, why don't we just call 911 and have 'em come over and patch him right up," Norm says.

I offer him a sarcastic smile. "It was an accident," I say. Then I turn to the large man, "I'm sorry, okay? I'm sorry. You just spooked us."

The big guy nods, tears in his eyes. The blubbering has calmed to a constant buzz, so I lean down and help him up. Behind the bar is a stack of clean rags. I lead him over to it and hand him a wad. He looks at the towels like he doesn't know what to do.

"Let's get you cleaned up," I say.

"It h-hurts," he answers.

"I know," I say. "I'm sorry."

I end up doing it for him the way I'd imagine my father would've done for me had he been around while I grew up. After a moment, the cries subside. So I say, "Do you know anything about Eden?"

This large black man looks at me as if I'm talking about ghosts.

15

"D-Don't take me back to Eden, mister. Please," the man says. He is sitting on a bar stool, the legs groaning and creaking under his weight.

Well, that's two strikes. Three strikes and we're out. It's looking more and more like Tony Richards wasn't as delusional as I thought. Eden might be lost, but that doesn't mean I won't fight for it.

"I'm not gonna take you back," I say, sticking out my hand. "I'm Jack, by the way, Jack Jupiter. This here is my older brother, Norm."

The man smiles. "I had a brother once. He was older, too! One time, he took me to the waterpark. I rode the slides until they closed! It was the best day ever!" He looks at his boots longingly.

Norm gives me that scrunched-brow look.

"That's very nice," I say. Obviously this guy is not

all there. I just hope my whack to his head wasn't the cause of it. "What is your name?"

"I'm Herbert. My friends call me Herb or Herbie. You can call me whatever you like! Just as long as you promise not to take me back." He looks up at me, eyes wide and shiny with tears. Man, it's a tough sight to see — a man this big, this scared. Looking at him, I wouldn't take him back now even if you paid me a million bucks.

I pat him on the shoulder. "No worries, Herb." There's a pause. "I am wondering, though, why don't you want to go back?"

Herb starts shaking his head. "Oh, it's terrible, Jacky. They make me do the worst things for Spike and his army. I have to touch the bodies. The dead ones that aren't really dead, like the movies, Jack. The movies! I have to cut their fingers off and remove their teeths. I don't like it. No, sir, I don't!"

I look at Norm, his lips parting as if to say something, but the door explodes open. Herb shrieks and almost falls off his stool, the bloody towels escaping his grip and landing wetly on the bar's floor.

My hands go for the Midnight Special in my waistband, but once I see it's Abby, they relax. She comes in with a broken pool stick in one hand. Darlene is not far behind her, holding the other end of the broken stick. When they see us, they relax. "What's going on? Everything okay? I heard Norm's gun — " Abby says.

"We're fine," I say. "Just made a new friend." I point at Herb and he smiles again. "His name is Herb and he's from Eden."

Abby's eyebrows arch at that.

"Go on, Herb," I say.

"Well they make — " Herb continues, but he is cut off by Darlene.

"There's a car! A car is coming!" she shouts, leaning out of the door. "It looks like an Army truck."

"Oh no, they found me! They found me! They're gonna make me scoop the rotten guts. Oh no oh no oh no — "

"Shush!" Norm says.

I rush over to Darlene, grab her around the waist and pull her inside. A bullet slams into the closing glass door seconds after I drag Darlene away.

Then someone speaks over a loudspeaker: "We know you're in there! Come out and we won't kill ya." But as if to contradict that very statement, the gun bursts again. Shit. Whoever is out there means business. Those were the shots of a sharpshooter. The bullets hit one of the many parked cars, thumping their metal bodies, breaking their windshields and windows. An alarm begins to go off, God knows how. Now Main Street in the small, Floridian town of Sharon is starting to sound like World War III.

16

Once the shooting stops, it's quiet and I pull the Midnight Special free. I'm sick of bloodshed, but I'll do what I have to do to protect my family.

The gunfire ripples through the air again.

The door to the bar shatters. Darlene screams. I roll away from the spray of glass and shield her with my skinny body.

"We aren't going to ask nicely again!" the voice from the loudspeaker booms.

Is this what they consider asking nicely?

"We're gonna start using the heavy artillery, Herb," the man says. "Just come out and we'll let you keep your fingers...most of them." Laughter erupts from the car, some of it caught over the speaker.

I shoot a glance at Herb. He is frozen still.

"It's the bad men," he says.

Norm stands up, I try to grab at his arm, but it's too late. He grabs the American flag off of its holder in the corner of the room, and sticks it out of the broken door.

"Norm," I say. "Get down."

I don't know these people, these madmen with guns and heavy artillery, but I know they *are* madmen. This ruined world's madmen will shoot you first and never consider asking questions. They don't care.

Thing is, I've always expected Norm to be a special kind of madman himself.

Case in point, him half sticking out of the door, his boots crunching the shards of glass as he waves the flag in some sort of truce.

"Surrender!" he yells. "We surrender."

"Herbert, that you?" Loudspeaker says.

"No! Name's Norman Jupiter. We don't want any trouble. We're just passing through."

"You're passing through our town, buddy," Loudspeaker replies. "You want to do that, you have to pay a toll."

I look at Herb. He moves like an animal caught in a trap, rocking back and forth on large boot heels. Frantic. Scared. It pains me to see him like that, so *defeated.* No human should ever have to feel like that.

I help Darlene up, her face is wet with tears, then I turn to Abby perched behind an overturned table. "Go," I say. "Out the back right now and hide until this is over. We'll meet up back at the clock we passed on the way here."

Abby shakes her head. She knows a storm is brewing. She hates being treated like this — shielded. I've seen what she did in Woodhaven, and I've seen what she's done in our travels. When the world began ending, she thrived. She's saved me on more than one occasion and now I mean to save her.

After some reluctance, she nods.

I grab Darlene and kiss her. "It'll be okay, I'll see you soon."

"Oh, Jack, just reason with them," Darlene says. "Maybe they can help us, too."

I don't tell her how unlikely that is. The type of people who shoot first and then call your name are not the type to reason with.

Abby takes the Midnight Special, and the two of them go out of the back.

"You got Herb in there?" Loudspeaker says. "You got him in there then we won't make you pay the toll."

Yeah, right, I think.

Norm ponders this question for a moment. A long moment.

"Well?" Loudspeaker asks.

Norm looks at Herb, their eyes meet. Terror in Herb's. Understanding in my older brother's.

"Tick, tock," Loudspeaker says. "Time's up."

We all drop. The machine gun goes off, drilling the

bar's facade. What was left of the windows break apart. Old, dusty bottles of Jack Daniels and Absolute Vodka explode. The mirror behind the bar disintegrates into almost nothing. Somehow, I think that's got to be more than seven years of bad luck for Loudspeaker and his gang outside.

Then the shots stop. All is quiet.

"Go check," Loudspeaker says, but not over the loudspeaker. It's so quiet, I hear it all.

"No, you go check," another voice responds.

"Don't be a pussy, Ramirez. They're dead, no one could survive that," Loudspeaker says. Even I can hear the uncertainty in the man's voice.

Norm looks at me. We nod, knowing what we have to do.

"No," Herb says. "Let me go out there. I will take my punishment." He holds his hand up studying his fingers.

"No," I say. "Don't be stupid. We can take them."

Outside, I hear the tentative footsteps of Ramirez coming to check on us. I risk a glance. He's carrying an AR15, something straight out of a video game. These guys definitely have the heavy artillery. Next thing you know they'll be lighting us up with a rocket launcher. All these weapons just laying around in this dead world, I guess someone had to take them.

The footsteps stop. This man with his AR15 is

scared of us. If only he knew what we're packing. He'd be laughing if he saw me with a dull machete.

"Step aside, I mean it," Herb says, his voice rumbling over a whisper.

The footsteps start again. Norm risks a glance over the window ledge, now minus its glass. A shadow dances on the wood panel walls — Ramirez's shadow — and this shadow raises its weapon.

Norm doesn't hesitate. He takes aim with his Magnum, and lets a bullet fly. The shadow on the wall disintegrates, but not before a burst sprays from the man's shoulder.

I drop behind the cover of the brick door frame, peeking around to see who's next.

There's no storm of bullets like I expect. There's just calm. Unsettling calm.

But it's broken as Loudspeaker talks. "Well, damn, the bastards shot Ramirez," he says. "Blew a fucking hole through his neck. Guess they mean business."

Someone else echoes his laugh.

"You think Ramirez dying is funny?" he asks whoever laughed, not bothering to depress the speaker's button.

The laughter is quickly cut off.

Norm gives me a look. It's a look I know well thanks to our travels on the road. It's the *Time to fuck shit up look* look.

I take a deep, shaky breath. Killing is not something I enjoy doing, it's something I have to do. Something I have to do for Darlene. To survive. I know these people won't give us a slap on the wrist. They're killers. We all are.

We *have* to be.

Norm aims for a man wearing a riot helmet. In the harsh sunlight, I can see the dried-on bits of brains and guts and blood on him.

In the past year I've gotten much better at shooting — especially compared to my time trapped in the Woodhaven Recreation Center — but Norm has gotten even better.

The soldier is only a young man.

I lean forward and grab Norm's arm. "No," I say and take the gun from him. He's smiling, probably thinking I'm craving blood.

That's not the case.

I'm saving the soldier's life. I'm saving all of our lives.

I take aim and shoot the truck bed, the bullet sparks off the metal with a *ding*. The guy with the helmet drops down, hiding and probably not realizing if the shot would have hit him, shattering his bloody visor into a million shards which would've blinded him, his movement would've been much too late.

Probably not realizing I spared him.

Whoever's driving the truck, someone I can't see due to the sun rays bouncing back at me from the glass, decides the last shot was too close to home, and puts it into reverse. Tires squeal, sending little puffs of white smoke into the air. The truck clips the backend of a Kia, busting both of their taillights and then turns around by jumping the curb, coming dangerously close to smashing in a coffee place that's a blatant ripoff of Starbucks, and heading in the direction they came.

Herb is still behind me. He watches them go, his lips quivering.

"We did it!" Norm says. "But your aim needs some work, little bro."

"Thanks. We can celebrate later. Let's go get Darlene and Abby," I say.

Norm waves a hand. "Oh, they're fine. Abby's a tough son of a — "

"Yeah, but Darlene isn't," I say, turning toward the back door.

17

THEY ARE BY THE CLOCK TOWER A FEW STREETS OVER. I wave at Abby, and we start walking toward them, keeping low to the derelict cars. We don't know who else could be lurking in Sharon's streets — dead or undead.

I look at them from the mouth of an alleyway, Norm, Herb, and a stinking trash can behind me. Herb has calmed down a little since our run in with Loudspeaker and his gang.

"Let's go," I start to say, but distant gunfire cuts me off. Not as distant as I need it to be.

Herb about falls down on the concrete and curls up into a ball.

Abby, a mere fifty feet away from us, raises her gun, Darlene slumping behind her. At the top of the street, where dead traffic lights sway in a gentle but hot

Florida breeze, I see the Army truck creeping through the intersection. One of the men wearing military camouflage and a riot helmet which sits on the top of his head stands up in the truck bed. He has a pair of binoculars up to his eyes, scanning the abandoned streets.

Abby and Darlene are quick to take cover behind the tall brick surface of the miniature clock tower.

"Jack," Norm whispers. I turn to see him pointing at the end of the alley. A zombie has spotted us. It sways back and forth, bouncing off the sides of the buildings. It is missing an arm, the yellowish bone hangs from the stump. Its neck cricks back and forth as if he is a malfunctioning robot.

"I got it," Norm says.

When Herb sees it, he shrieks out, and Herb is a big man, though he may not act like it. His shriek is earth-shaking. I shove a hand over his mouth, though I think it's too late. His skin is somehow cold and clammy in this ridiculous heat.

I glance around the brick's corner. The truck is stopped. Loudspeaker gets out of the driver's side.

"Herbert Walker, this is your last chance!"

Herb makes a move, but I push him back against the bricks. It's not hard. He doesn't put up a fight. Behind me, I hear the squish of Norm dashing the zombie's brains, then the corpse falling to the concrete.

"We will forgive you for your crimes of conspiracy.

You will serve a small sentence. Nothing harsh. You will not be executed if you comply," Loudspeaker continues.

I shake my head at Herb. "Don't believe them," I whisper. "Don't believe a damn thing."

I catch another's voice. "More coming, boss," a female says, then the microphone clicks off.

"Should we fight?" Norm asks.

I shake my head again. No, not yet. We can get out of this without bloodshed. There's enough of that going around.

I jump as a horn blares. One deep blast from the truck, then another. Feedback crackles from the speaker. The Eden man says, "All right, Herb, if that's the way you want it to be." The horn sounds again. "That's right, come on, you grimy bastards," he is saying. He's not talking to us. I see Abby and Darlene staring at me with wide eyes. Loudspeaker holds something like a stick of dynamite in his hands. I'm about to shit my pants. This crazy bastard is going to blow us all to hell. The first of the dead shamble through the intersection, their arms outstretched, their head nothing more than thin, gray skin pasted over a skull.

I am not relieved to find out it isn't a stick of dynamite in Loudspeaker's hands. He yanks the top part of the stick off and then strikes it against what looks like his fist. It's now I realize what it actually is.

It's a flare, and bright, fiery sparks of red fly out of it. Loudspeaker throws it down the street, and this man must've been a professional quarterback because he almost makes it to the clock tower. It's not a crazy far throw, but it's a decent distance. It bounces off of the road, still shooting flames and sparks that are somehow brighter than the Florida sun.

"Oh, shit," I say as the leading zombie turns his direction toward the flare and us beyond it. We have to go.

I wave Abby down despite her looking at me fiercely. I point behind me. "Let's go," I mouth.

She looks a little apprehensive, and Darlene is basically frozen to the ground, but Abby grabs her arm and pulls.

The two begin to move across the street, low to the ground.

A gunshot goes off. Bullets clobber the asphalt, digging up chunks of black rock and dust.

"Oh no oh no oh no," Herb says behind me.

I hear a slap then Norm saying, "Get a hold of yourself and stop bleeding!" but it's a distant echo because I'm already in the street, shielding Darlene and Abby from the bullets with my thin body. It is probably not the best idea, but what choice do I have? I cannot stand and watch them be cut down.

I won't let that happen. I would rather die instead.

I push them, my fingers digging into their arms, not

on purpose, and I spur them forward, then dive the rest of the way as more bullets whine off the sidewalk, and an entire brick is taken out of the corner of the building next to me.

The shots stop, and the snarls pound my eardrums. I don't look again because I know what's coming. It's a wave of zombies. They have started to hunt in packs, started to roll through the towns and fields like ravaging tornadoes. They are hungry.

They are always hungry.

I don't know the layout of this abandoned town called Sharon. I do know we have no choice but to run.

I take the lead, my hand gripping Darlene's for dear life. Abby hands me the gun. Norm, her, and Herb are behind Darlene and I. We have two guns, but they are not good guns, though any gun is good in a zombie apocalypse, I guess. But in close quarters like this, something you have to reload is never a good thing. There are definitely more zombies than there are bullets between us.

We are heading back to the bar. cutting through another alley, weaving between piles of discarded trash that will never be picked up.

Two zombies block the end of the alley which spills out on Main Street. I raise my gun, the little Midnight Special, and blow their heads clean off. I don't even see where I'm aiming as much as I *feel* where I'm aiming. I am no Jedi, I have no Force powers. I am just experienced.

I *am* Johnny Deadslayer.

The two zombies were once citizens of this town, I have no doubt. One wears a tattered skirt and a frilly, flowery blouse. She must've been the librarian or perhaps worked in the used book store across from the bar. The other is a man, the type of man you'd find working the nine-to-five at a factory then working his whiskey from five-to-one at the town watering hole. His beard is long, streaked with blood. I do this sometimes, give the zombies back stories, try to remember what their lives were like before they were mindless monsters, and sometimes it's even more detailed, especially when I'm scared. Sometimes it helps, too, but other times it makes things worse. Harder. Darlene screams. Norm is grunting, pumping his legs, and Abby is cool and calm, dragging Herb along with us.

I hear the dead behind me, I don't know how far, but that is enough to know I don't have time to be scared. I have to protect my family, get us back to safety. Without my family, I am nothing. I am just another statistic, another loner who ate a bullet when things turned really bad.

I don't want that.

I want to live.

The body of the military man who Norm shot is not in the same spot as he was when we left the bar.

He is there.

And here.

There, too.

It's like the zombies tore him apart and took their meals to go.

Then, tires squeal. A cloud of smoke puffs from the back of the truck as it turns the corner on Main, mowing down a couple zombies in the process. The body of the truck jumps a bit as it does this, fishtails on the blood, then rights itself.

We are standing in the middle of the street.

Another horde is coming down at us from my right. Not enough as the one behind us, but enough to make running through any of these places an act of insanity.

We are surrounded.

Fuck. I've failed.

Failed my family.

Norm sees all of this before I do. He does that sometimes. He can scope out enemies, formations, he can read people, too — it's quite a talent.

I know he sees this before I do because his gun is drawn. He fires three quick shots at the Army truck's windshield. It is not going fast, but it is going and it is coming right for us.

The bullets whine off of the metal. One hits the glass. It doesn't shatter and the driver, who I can only make out as a vague, helmet-wearing figure, doesn't even flinch.

These are people who have their shit together, the types of people who used to read books on apocalypse prepping, who sat around the dinner table and talked about zombie evacuation plans. The people everyone laughed at. Bulletproof glass. Armor. AR15s.

We are out of our element. Over-gunned. Outmatched.

Fucked.

Norm doesn't bother to fire again.

He looks to me, our eyes reading each other's thoughts almost perfectly. It was something we did as kids, lost for fifteen years since we have been apart, and now found again in this fucked-up world.

I am the first to lay my gun down and stick my hands up in the air. Norm is the second. The rest follow.

"It's okay," I say, my voice calm and steady, a perfect opposition to how I feel on the inside. Darlene whimpers. I look at her. Sweat is running down her forehead, tears from her eyes. "It'll be okay," I say, and she nods.

I step in front of Darlene, putting my body between her and the unspeakable evil that comes at us from all sides.

18

LOUDSPEAKER GETS OUT OF THE TRUCK FIRST. HE IS wearing a full-body camouflage suit, boots and all. He does not have a beard like most of the people I've seen roaming this wasteland. This is a man that not only accepts that the world has ended, but revels in it.

Two others get out of the cabin, and another from the truck bed. Four people in all. They all wear military outfits, too. One of them is a girl, but she's muscular, wiry, not the type of girl who takes shit from people.

My group...well, we are a lousy bunch in comparison. For one, Loudspeaker's group has weapons and cars, and it looks as if they'd had an honest-to-God meal every day, and a shower, too.

I should probably quit calling him Loudspeaker

because he no longer has it in hand. Maybe I should call him Asshole or Military Douchebag.

"Ready, boys?" he asks his crew, leaning his head to one side and speaking over his shoulder.

"Sir, yes, sir!" they answer in unison. All of their voices sound exactly alike. I can't even pick out the female's.

"Fire!"

Just like that, I think as they raise their assault rifles.

Darlene lets out a little shriek. Herb hits the ground behind me.

Just like that. I don't even get a chance to beg God for forgiveness. Blink, and you're dead.

I close my eyes, expecting to be riddled with holes.

Rat-tata-tata-tata-tata...rat-tata-tata-tata.

I don't fall to the ground like everyone else. I stand. I take it, tensing my body pointlessly in preparation of the bullets that will end my life.

The shooting stops.

I look down, expecting to see blood and smoking wounds.

Nothing.

I pat myself a few times, turn my head around and see everyone else is still alive. I want to fall on my knees and cry and thank God, but I don't.

With the Jugheads' arrival — *Jugheads*, that's what

I'll call them now — I had forgotten about the ever-present threat of the zombies.

Now, that threat is gone.

I turn around to look at the dead who were slowly making their way to us. They are nothing but heaps of twisted meat, scalps peeled off, features distorted not only by rot but by bullets, too.

"Missed one," Loudspeaker says.

"Got it, sir!" the female answers. She brings her assault rifle up, squints one almond-shaped eye, and looks down the sight. A shot bursts to my left and a zombie's head goes with it.

"Fine shooting, Rockwell."

"Thank you, sir!" she answers.

I also want to thank her, but I know that would be stupid.

"Great, now that is over, I'd like to have a proper interaction with you clowns, understood?" the man formerly known as Loudspeaker says.

None of us answer, we are just staring at him with fear, anger, hate, and misplaced gratitude on our faces.

"All right, not the most talkative bunch, I see. Well then, I am Butch Hazard, and seeing as how I just saved your asses, I'd think it's fair enough for you to save mine."

Again, we stay quiet.

Screw you, Butch Hazard. Screw you and your weapons and your soldiers.

Butch Hazard nods. "I see you ain't a polite bunch, either. That's okay. We can fix that, can't we, soldiers?"

"Sir, yes, sir!" they answer again in unison.

"Put a bullet in the skinny blonde bitch's head. I don't care if you shoot that man in front of her, either," Butch Hazard says.

What? No.

They raise their weapons just like they talk.

I break the silence. This has gone too far. I will rip each of their heads off before I let them harm the love of my life.

I don't care if I die.

"Stop this," I say.

"Oh, he talks, does he?" Butch Hazard says.

His 'soldiers' laugh together, sounding exactly alike.

"Good to know we ain't dealing with muties here," he says. "Now, let's talk business."

"We don't want to do business," I say. I would do business with the Devil before I did business with a bunch of jackasses holding us at gunpoint.

"You don't have a choice."

"There's always a choice," I answer back.

"No, there's not," Butch says. "Not when you're staring down the barrel of five guns. I can make you think there's a choice, sure, but I think we're passed that, don't you?"

"Oh, fuck off!" Abby says from my side. She is not

hidden behind Norm. She is not afraid, at least not visibly. "This isn't your world. This is no one's world but the dead's. You don't make the rules."

Butch Hazard starts to laugh. "'No one's world but the dead's,' I like that. Girl's got a mouth on her," he says, then tilts his head and gives her a wink. "But do you know how to use it the right way?"

"Shut your fucking mouth," I say.

Norm makes a move for his gun, but the clicking sounds of the rifles ring out, and he pauses.

"Listen," Butch Hazard says. "I don't want to shoot you, I really don't, so let's cut to the chase. You have something *I* want and *we* have something *you* want."

"Yeah," I say, "and what's that?"

"We have your freedom, the ability to let you walk away from this situation without another scratch. The path is clear, the dead are dead, and you can get to safety before more arrive," Butch says. "So you give us Herbert, and then we can all get on with our lives." He smiles, a big, toothy grin.

"No," I say, my mind made up. "I've seen what that place did to Herb. He doesn't want to go back so he's not going back. Simple. End of story."

Darlene squeezes me. She's not telling me I made the wrong choice. Darlene would support me if I said we all need to stop eating old junk food and start dining on the millions of zombies roaming around. No, she's squeezing me because she's scared. A natural reflex for fear.

I feel it, too. We all do. It hangs in the air like a heavy rain cloud, ready to burst.

"That's not how it works," Butch says. There's a flash of anger in his eyes. "Spike gets to say who comes and who goes. And Herbert was not on the list. Herbert belongs in Eden."

"Herbert can do whatever he damn-well pleases," I say, then look at Herb. He's shaking, the large muscles beneath the layers of his flesh dancing. "Do you want to go with Mr. Butch Hazard, here, Herb?"

He shakes his head, slowly, deliberately.

"There," I say, "the man has spoken. And last I heard, it was a free country."

Butch Hazard walks closer to where we stand, but he is still a good twenty yards away. His fingers hook his belt loops, and he leans back and laughs.

"In case you haven't noticed," he says, "this ain't a country no more. Freedom's gone. Now I'm a man of good morals, that much is true. I say my prayers every night, wash my hands before every meal, and kiss my wife goodbye whenever I leave our compound, so I'm all about freedom and free choice and countries and all that hippie bullshit. But don't get me started on freedom. *True* freedom. I damn near died for the freedom of this country more than once." He laughs as he pulls the collar of his shirt down, revealing a puckered scar that can be none other than a scarred over bullet wound. “This is just one, got a couple more on my back and thigh, but I’ll hope you take my word for it. So don’t talk to me about freedom.”

“I don’t want to go back,” Herb says. His voice is hardly a whisper. I barely hear it and I don’t think anyone else does.

“Now you don’t want the extinction of the human race on your hands, do you?” Butch Hazard asks me. His eyes drilling down into my soul. They are as black as onyx, as emotionless as a zombie.

“What the fuck are you talking about?” Norm asks. He leans forward, his eyes narrowed. I know he’s fallen for the trap. Butch threw out the bait and he’s trying to hook us. I won’t fall for it. I know this shit is too deep to get out of. The human race is nothing but a dwindling flame. By next year, it’ll be a spark, and depending how you look at it, that spark can easily blow out at the first strong breeze.

“I’m talking about Eden and I’m talking about Herbert Walker,” Butch says. “This dumb-looking bastard is the key to us beating these suckers. In Eden, we are doing something great. We are coming up with a cure. We are fixing this fuck-up.” He points to the dead on my left.

All I can think is *bullshit*. I wouldn’t believe anything this guy says.

“I’m not going!” Herb says, a repeat of his earlier

sentiment, but this time his voice is louder. One of Butch's soldiers breaks formation. It's the slightest movement, but I see it, and I sense that Abby sees it too by the way she looks in the man's direction.

"Oh ho ho," Butch says, "look who learned how to speak up."

"I don't wanna work for him no longer," Herb says. "I don't wanna help."

"Well, see, Herb, that's the conundrum we're in here. I *do* work for Spike, and I have my orders."

Butch reaches behind his back, pulls a pistol free. Sunlight catches on the chrome, momentarily blinding me.

"My orders are simple. Bring Herb back, bring anyone who leaves the compound back, and kill whoever gets in our way if I have to. I'm gonna do just that," Butch says, striding the rest of the way over to us.

I reach for the gun on the ground. Fuck this. I'm sick of listening to lies. Kill or be killed. Johnny Deadslayer.

"And I really don't want you bleeding all over my truck, Herb," Butch finishes.

He pulls the trigger of the pistol. A bullet strikes the road, taking a chunk of the yellow line with it, and sending my Midnight Special careening out of reach.

"Don't be a hero, kid," he says to me. "Take your girls and your friend here and get the hell out of Sharon before I have to kill you all."

I am wise enough to back up. Without a weapon, I am useless and Darlene is dead.

Unfortunately, Norm is not as wise as me. He never has been. He's a hothead...I think I've mentioned that before.

He grabs his gun, drops to his knees, and rolls to the side. His gun goes off, missing Butch. It whines off of the truck's bulletproof windshield. The soldiers raise their weapons and for a moment, I think I see their muzzles flashing and I think I hear the roars. But they don't.

They don't have permission.

This is Butch's fight now.

He raises his pistol.

"Norm — " but the bark of the gun cuts me off.

It's all in slow motion. The finger squeezing, the slide jerking back, the explosion from the barrel, and finally the bullet slicing through the air and burying itself into Norm's leg. It hits him hard enough to drive him over the curb, where he lands among the dead zombies.

I start to run toward him, but Darlene grabs me. We look at each other, and the look she gives me is one of defeat, her eyes drooping, mouth a thin line.

"Next one is going in his skull," Butch Hazard says. I am surprised at how steady his voice is. He looks at us, and a wave of rage grips me. I'm shaking, I feel the heat pulsing through my body. "Now, Herbert, let's go."

"No," I say. "You're a man of morals, right?"

Butch narrows his eyes at me, but there's a smile on his face. He is in a jovial mood, I think. I doubt anyone ever opposes him.

He doesn't answer immediately. Instead, he points the pistol at me, and raises his other hand to the soldiers behind him. It's a signal. I know this because they all raise their assault rifles. "When I'm on the clock, I'm anything I have to be," he says.

As I stare down the barrels of five guns, I realize I really need to start keeping my mouth shut.

19

Next thing I know, I'm on my knees, but I'm not begging for my life. There is only one gun aimed on me, and it's Butch's. He has waved his soldiers down, said, "No, I want to do this myself," and here I am, shaking...with fear, with rage.

Darlene is sobbing.

"Ooh, Spike is gonna like you," Butch says. "The mouthy one, too."

Abby grabs Darlene and pulls her away from me. But Darlene has a handful of my shirt, and she rips a piece of the fabric free.

All my muscles tense. I feel like I am drowning, like I am in a nightmare and I'm trying to run but getting nowhere.

Butch laughs.

All this time, I'm not worrying about myself, about

the bullet about to be lodged in my brain — that is, if Butch is feeling generous, but I doubt it, I'll just wind up bleeding out like a stuck pig while the zombies follow the noise and devour me. I don't care if that's the case. All I care about is Darlene getting away, of Norm living through this, and Abby being able to grow up. She's only nineteen.

"I would've turned my back on this whole situation if you would've given me Herb." Butch shakes his head. "Now, that would've been the wisest choice, my friends. If you went that route, I wouldn't have to blow your heads off."

"Fuck you," Norm says. He is weak, barely hanging on.

Butch laughs again. "I love the fight, really. It's admirable."

He looks at me, stares down the sight. I am sweating. The gun is cool against my skin.

"Any last words?"

"Fuck you," I say, echoing Norm.

"Wrong answer."

I close my eyes, it's not a sign of weakness. It's more of a reflex. Preparation for my brains to be blown out.

And a shot goes off, but it's not as loud as I think.

Then I hear screaming. A man screaming, but gurgling as well, as if a great monster is dragging him into the ocean's depths.

I open my eyes, my jaw drops at what I see.

Butch Hazard is distracted. Everyone is.

One of the soldiers, the one wearing sunglasses with a goatee, has dropped his assault rifle. He clutches at a burning hole in his throat. Blood spurts from between his fingers. The other soldiers watch him, their faces distorted with fear and confusion, but they won't break rank anymore than they have.

Another shot follows. This one is much closer, I can practically hear the bullet *whoosh* by my head. A couple inches to the left and I'd be missing a chunk of my scalp. Butch jerks at the exact moment of the second shot.

He's good.

He anticipated the bullet slamming into his chest, and by jerking, it only managed to clip his shoulder. There's a small spray of blood then the slug thumping into the Army truck.

I wish it would've hit him in the heart. Doesn't matter. He is momentarily distracted. Now's our chance.

I turn to Darlene and grab her. Abby, helps me to my feet. "Go!" I say.

We have a guardian angel. We can run and never look back.

"What about you?" Abby says.

"I got Norm."

She nods, and joins Herb into helping Darlene to

her feet. They clear the street just as another shot hits the truck, dinging the metal, causing it to rock.

Norm is crawling toward us, but it's not easy-going with one hand clamped over his thigh.

Another shot rings out.

Another soldier falls.

The others of Butch's army have their assault rifles aimed, sweeping the town beyond. Not shooting because they don't know where these shots are coming from.

Butch doesn't even look in our direction. He raises the hand up that holds his pistol to shield his eyes from the sun. He has taken cover behind one of the open truck doors, peeking through the glass.

Two more shots, and two more soldiers fall. All that is left is him and the female.

I grab Norm around the waist, try to help him to his feet.

"Hide all you want," Butch bellows. "Or come down and face me like a man, you pussy!" He aims in the general direction of the shots and lets loose a couple of his own. Down the street is a couple of higher buildings. A perfect sniper's nest.

Norm and I make our way across the street. "Fuck," he says. "I could use some of that booze."

"You better kill me now!" Butch screams. "If I find you I'm going to f— "

The female soldier finally breaks rank. She throws

the truck's door open just as a bullet hammers into the metal. Then she dives inside, taking cover behind the dashboard.

Norm and I are almost to Abby when Butch shoots again. This time at me.

All of a sudden my arm is on fire. It's like something has bitten me, has clamped their big, serrated teeth around my forearm and won't let go. My heart stops for a second as I think of a zombie using my forearm as a chew toy, but we are not by any zombies. We are in the middle of the street, and when I look down at the flaring pain, I don't see a rotting skull. I see blood and a fresh bullet wound. The bullet came from Butch's gun. The bastard has shot me.

Darlene must see this, must see me grabbing my arm like it's about to detach, because she breaks free from Abby's grip and runs out to meet us halfway in the road like I had done no less than twenty minutes ago to shield her and Abby from this bastard Butch Hazard's bullets.

Butch Hazard is a blur. He moves across the street like a black cloud filled with lightning. Darlene is out of my hands before I can even fully grasp her. She screams.

I scream.

Then there's a gun to her head and tears running down her face. "Jack!" she yells.

"You want to shoot me, you'll have to shoot both of us," Butch says to the empty street.

There is no gunshot.

But my rage, the fireworks inside of my head, are loud enough to drown out any gun. I rush him, leaving Norm where he is.

Butch holds the gun to Darlene's temple, one arm tucked under her chin as if he's putting her in a sleeper hold. She's still screaming, but the sound is muted and choked out.

I am about five feet away from them when I stop.

"No, not any farther," he says. "Fucking crazy bastard. You're just as bad as the dead, all of you! Thinking this was gonna be an easy day, boy, am I — "

He's cut off by a scream. It takes me a moment to realize the scream comes from his mouth. Darlene thrashes in his grip. I see her mouth gushing with red. Blood wells from little grooves in Butch's Hazard's flesh.

"Fuckin bitch!" he screams, but he let's go.

The sun is blazing and the picture is crystal clear — Ultra HD. She has bitten him in the soft spot of skin between his index finger and his thumb on his left hand. I see it all. The pink tendons, a flash of white bone, and blood. Lots of blood.

Darlene breaks free, and she's smart enough to not run toward me this time. She takes off in the direction of Abby and Herbert.

Norm is hobbling in that direction, leaving a trail of red behind as he does so. “Come on, Jack,” he says. “Let’s get the fuck — ”

But the fireworks in my head don’t let him finish that sentence. The way I see Butch Hazard is the way I saw Freddy and Pat Huber, the way I see the millions of zombies who roam around and threaten my family each day.

I see them as bullies.

I don’t take shit from bullies anymore.

I rush Butch Hazard. Me, a kid from the now deceased Woodhaven, Ohio, versus some crazy war general with a chip on his shoulder and murder in his eyes.

It doesn’t matter. I’ve made up my mind.

I start with a kick. It’s not a powerful kick by any means, but it doesn’t have to be. My booted foot clobbers his kneecap. Something snaps and crackles as Butch stumbles and falls to the concrete behind the truck’s open door. The gun scatters across the road. I follow it’s trajectory for a moment, then look back to Butch.

Inside the truck, I hear whimpering. The female soldier is on the floor between the dashboard and the seats. Her gun is for the taking, and she is too scared and distracted.

I reach for it, my hands barely brushing the metal as —

Big mistake.

Rage has caused me to underestimate my opponent.

Butch Hazard grabs my ankle and he twists. Blood from his bite wound sprays in a mist, rotates with the turn. I hear a pop. Then I'm falling and eating asphalt. I hit the ground hard enough to make me wheeze. Ribs I hurt almost a year ago from my fall off the roof of the Woodhaven Rec Center burn with pain.

Butch Hazard stands over me. I don't know how he stands, but he does. His eyes bug out from his face, bloodshot, filled with rage and agony, a fire I've never seen in my life, nor do I want to ever see again.

The pain in my arm, my shot arm, is burning something fierce.

"You're gonna have to kill me!" Butch shouts.

I don't know if he's shouting at me.

I'm hoping, praying, wishing for whoever is shooting from the buildings behind me to shoot one time.

One more damn time.

But sometimes, you have to do things on your own. You can't wait for things to fix themselves.

And if I'm going to die, I'm going to die fighting.

20

Both fortunately and unfortunately, my older brother won't let me do it.

Norm is on me before I can throw my last punch. He barrels into Butch Hazard. Butch is not a large man, he is just one that refuses to fall over.

I pull myself up, getting ready to fight.

We might both be shot, we might both be scared, and in Norm's case, a little hungover, but Butch doesn't stand a chance against the Jupiter brothers.

That much I am sure.

I get ready to rush at him when I see the glare of headlights. The remaining soldier is behind the wheel.

The truck is coming right for us.

Two shots ring out from a distance. Dead accurate shots. If the windshield wasn't bulletproof, the woman would be missing most of her face.

Everything is moving in slow motion. Darlene's cries for me are warped and watery. Norm's are not, pained shouts of war. Butch grunts.

All the while, I wonder how I got myself into this situation.

Slow motion off.

Fast forward on.

The truck flies down the road at what seems like a million miles per hour. I dive out of the way, leaving my brother behind. There's no time to grab him and pull him with me.

Butch swings, his fist connecting meatily with Norm's face. My brother staggers, feigns a punch, then falls over. He is out cold. Butch Hazard has a mean right hook.

The truck stops about two feet short from Norm's head.

Slow motion again.

I am in a dream, pumping my legs as fast as I can, but getting nowhere. Each step I get closer to Norm, he gets farther and farther away until the truck is blocking my view. It whooshes in front of me so fast that I stumble and fall on my ass, half on the curb, half on the road. It's painful now, and I barely feel it because of the adrenaline and fear pumping through my veins, but I'll really feel it later.

Fast forward.

I hear the squeal of the tires, the distant snarls

from the dead. Darlene behind me says my name over and over again. "Jack, Jack, Jack! Come on!"

The door slams. I see a blur of a bloody face, but it belongs to a monster. The beaming sun hits me in the eyes. This monster is not a monster, it's just a conglomeration of Butch and Norm. Butch has Norm over his shoulders. He dumps my older brother's limp body into the truck's cabin.

Then they're gone, the tires squealing, rifle shots chasing after them, thumping the metal, whining off the asphalt.

No slow motion this time. Just me and the road. I spring up, hardly noticing the pain all over my body. My legs fire up the street, weaving in and out of dead and mutilated zombies, almost slipping in their blood and guts.

But I am not fast enough.

I stop, fall over, feeling my lungs burn, feeling my small dinner of peanuts and flat Coca-Cola threaten to come out of me. I look up at the taillights of the truck, see them getting smaller and smaller.

I swear I see Norm's hand, his bloody hand, smear the back window, and my heart breaks.

It's too late. I've failed.

21

Darlene's small hands reach under my armpits, but she is too weak to lift me off of the road. It takes all three of them — Herb, Abby, and Darlene.

I have lost one of the last anchors of my old life. My older brother who I grew up with, who I share my most fondest and most terrible memories with is now gone. This is my fault. All my fault.

My family is like table legs. If you take one away, the table is no longer sturdy. It's falling, no longer a table, no longer whole. I cannot face this dead world without my older brother. We will topple over without him.

I can't even stand up straight. I might be crying, I'm not sure. Something is stinging my eyes, either tears or sweat.

"Norm," I say, feeling the lump in my throat.

"We gotta go," Abby says. "They were shooting. They could — "

"They weren't shooting at us. They were helping us," I say. My voice sounds angry to my own ears, but I'm not the best judge. They all look at me like I'm crazy, and right at this moment, I feel fucking crazy.

"Come on," Darlene says.

"No, we have to get Norm," I say.

"Not now," Abby says. "You're hurt and not in your right mind, Jack, but we will get him back. We will, I promise."

I've been shot. It's this realization, this mental acceptance that I've been shot which brings the pain. Terrible bursts of pain. Have you ever been shot? It's worse than anything a dentist can do to you with their tray of sharp torture tools, worse than any doctor with his colonoscopy kit.

"I'm sorry, kid," a voice says. It's one I recognize, but not one I'd ever think of hearing again. I turn around and I am face to face with Tony Richards. His son is next to him. Tony carries the sniper rifle with its large scope, the same one I saw back on the farm. The gun hangs over his shoulders on straps."I tried so damn hard to brain that son of a bitch," he says.

"If it wasn't for you two, it could've been so much worse," I say.

Tony comes over and grips my good arm. "It'll be okay," he says.

"How do you know?" I ask.

"Because we have him on our side," Tony replies. He is pointing at Herb. Herb's eyes go wide, his mouth works like he is trying to swallow his tongue. "Herb here is on the inside, I'm sure he told you. He knows all the inner workings of the compound, the secret tunnels, the schedules. Don't you Herb?" Tony asks.

Herb looks down at his feet, and shakes his head. "I don't wanna go back," he says. "Don't make me — "

Darlene pats him. "Shh, it's okay. Don't worry," she says.

"Herb knows it ain't okay. Don't sugarcoat it, darling. You don't know Butch Hazard. He would've done worse than you could possibly imagine to you and yours, and he would just be the appetizer. The main course would be Spike, and he'd pull your teeth out one by one with dirty needle-nosed pliers, digging into the gums and all, not caring about how loud you scream. Then he'll cut your fingers off. He likes that for some reason."

Darlene shakes her head, continues patting Herb.

"You got off a lot easier than you think," Brian says to Darlene. Then he looks at me. "Don't think I haven't lost people, too."

"Now, let's get that wound cleaned up," Tony says, squinting at the bloody mess on my arm.

"We got a lot of medical shit back at the house," Brian says. When he says this, I have another realization. This is a man who is barely a man. He might be eighteen or in his twenties, but under that scruffy, patchy beard, he is just a kid. His adult life will be short. All of our lives will be. Instead of banks and bills and groceries, date night with the missus, raising kids, and the whole nine yards, Brian Richards will be fighting zombies, running for his life, struggling for food. It's a thought that saddens me. Abby is the same way. Her father will never walk her down the aisle, her mother will never help her pick out her wedding dress.

As if on cue, Abby looks at Brian, smiles and says, "Great way to put it…'medical shit'."

"You can help him? You swear?" Darlene asks.

"I'll do my best to help your husband, ma'am. Just like he helped me," Tony says.

She nods gratefully. I wonder what is going through her mind, whether she thinks I'll actually die from a bullet graze or the fact that her and I never actually got married. We are perpetually engaged. There are not many working chapels these days nor are there many places where I can drop a bunch of money on a wedding ring.

"Besides," Tony says, "I think I owe all of you guys one." He turns to face us again. The bottom of his eyes are wet, threatening tears. "You were right, Jack. I can't keep living in the past. There is hope in the future."

Brian puts his open hand on the back of his father's

neck and gives a little squeeze. Tony's hand settles on top of his son's.

"They are in a better place now. It was selfish of me to keep them around like that," he says.

I can only nod. The anger and shock in my head is all but fizzling out, replaced by sadness. A deep, painful sadness not only for the Richards family, but for this world in general.

I think of Norm, then, and a man named Spike, cutting his fingers off, torturing him.

22

WE GET BACK TO THE FARMHOUSE IN WHAT I WOULD consider a blur. I blame fatigue and shock and all sorts of other emotions I never want to feel again.

Somehow, we all stuffed into the Richards's Dodge. I actually had to sit on Darlene's lap because she refused to sit on mine because of my injuries. Screw emasculation, it was comfortable. Brian had a handkerchief in his back pocket. He tied it tight around the wound on my arm and confirmed that it was just a graze and I'd heal fine with the proper stitching and ointment application. He also told me he wrapped the wound with the side he doesn't blow his nose on, then he gave me a wink.

I didn't laugh. That was not a time for laughter.

Now, as I climb out of the Challenger, looking at the farmhouse's roof where my brother had puked off the side, I do laugh. There is no humor in the laugh. It is the laughter of a man whose insanity has been hanging on by a thread and who has just realized that thread has snapped.

I laugh so hard, it hurts my stomach. I laugh so hard, more blood spurts from the wound on my arm.

Darlene gets out after me. She is concerned, she is always concerned.

“Come on, let’s get him into the house,” Tony says.

Someone grabs my arm and ushers me up the front steps.

The sunshine is gone, no longer roasting my skin, warming me, and I’m in the house, which is considerably cooler but still stuffy. I feel a sense of claustrophobia creeping up my throat as if I am choking.

Brian guides me to the same kitchen table where we had our first meeting — at gunpoint — not even a day ago, but that time I had Norm with me. Even if he was a little drunk, I still felt better. This time, my arm is burning, I am suffering from insanity, and my brother is nowhere to be seen.

“Lay your arm down,” Brian says.

I do.

He starts to work at the knot of the handkerchief. Soon, Darlene is at my side. She says, “You can squeeze my hand if you want. This might hurt a little, honey.” She uses the sweet voice that she always uses when she wants something, or when she wants to prepare me for bad news.

Tony rummages in the other room, throwing pots and pans and junk and books around like he's a dog digging a hole in loose dirt. "Got it," he says. "That brother of his didn't drink all of it." His voice wavers in my ears.

I feel like I am falling. I feel like a failure.

I remember Ryan, the janitor at the Woodhaven Rec Center, screaming and crying as Miss Fox poured peroxide on his wound. Granted, his wound was much deeper, but that doesn't do much to calm me down.

"Herb, I'ma need you to hold him," Brian says. He reaches his hand out to grab the clear bottle. When he pops the cap off, a smell of pure, diesel-grade alcohol explodes from the mouth. I'm talking about the type of shit you pour into jet engines. It snaps me out of whatever fugue state I'm in. I see more clearly, think more clearly. It's a miracle really, and a bit ironic because if I took a sip of that stuff, I'd be worse off than I was before.

"Darlene," I say.

She looks at me, her face bunched up.

I hold out my hand. "I'll take it now," I say.

She smiles, and we lock hands.

"How cute," Tony says, then, "Herb, come on," as he points to my arm on the table. Herb is apprehensive. A big man trying to hide in the shadows and not doing a very good job, but he steps forward. His large hands pin my arm down at the elbow.

"Glad you asked for my permission," I say to him. His eyes widen. "No, I'm just kidding," I say.

"Ready?" Brian asks.

"Do your worst."

He pours the alcohol on the wound. I scream so hard, my lungs burn. My knees clatter against the underside of the table and despite Herb putting all his weight on it, it still lifts up about six inches. Abby puts a hand over my mouth. I feel the skin around the wound bubbling and fizzing like one of those science fair baking soda and vinegar volcanoes.

Then, it's over.

Brian is patting my arm with a bleach-white towel. The skin is numb. I wouldn't know he was doing that if my eyes weren't bugged out of my head. Tony produces a small, black leather bag and a pair of reading glasses from a case in his back pocket. He puts them on the end of his nose. He has never looked more like an old man than he does now. I'm just waiting for him to fall over and break his hip.

Help! I've fallen and I can't get up! Like those weird infomercials of the old world we all used to laugh at. I'd give anything to see one of those commercials again. Give anything for it to be three in the morning, Darlene sleeping in the room next to me, her soft snores acting as a soundtrack to the muted television playing while I finally finish that damn werewolf book I left back in Woodhaven. I know it'll never happen, but a guy can dream, can't he? Maybe even continue Johnny Deadslayer's tale with all this real-life inspiration.

Tony sticks me with a sewing needle and I barely feel it at all. I have no idea how Norm could've drank a whole bottle of this liquor and not died.

"Are you okay?" Darlene asks.

Abby removes her hand from my mouth, thank God.

"Yeah," I say, spitting a little, "I don't feel a thing!"

"I think you can let go of Jack there, Herb," Brian says. "The absinthe seems to have done the trick. Ain't nothing like it, I tell ya. Dad should've sold it to hospitals all over the world. We'd be millionaires. Not that it matters anymore..." he trails off.

"Yeah, and airports, too. Goodbye gas and oil crisis," I say.

This garners a few laughs from the group. Nervous laughs. Real laughter in this dead world is hard to come by.

"No, I'll stick to drinking it," Tony says after a moment of prolonged silence. He reaches out, grabs the bottle and swigs the last gulp.

"Do you think you should be drinking while you're sewing up my fiancé?" Darlene asks.

Tony nods. "Helps steady the hands." Then he's back to work. Stitching me up and me not feeling it.

"Do you think we should really be sewing me up when my brother is out there with Major Asshole?" I say.

More chuckles, bleeding closer and closer to real laughter.

"I'm serious," I say.

"Son, you rush into Eden, even at full strength, they will eat you alive," Tony says. "You would've gotten here six months ago when society was still kinda running and before Butch and Spike took over, you'd be looking at totally different story. You would've gotten a hot meal every night, the finest medical care, a warm bed to share with your lovely gal here, and whatever else you wanted, but not no more."

We hadn't heard about Eden six months ago, or believe me, we would've been there. Of course, there are other places with the same promises as Eden. Places where the walls were high and the ammunition was endless. They would let us in because Norm was a much needed soldier, in the raging zombie war. But those places are usually overrun, the fences collapsed, the buildings burned to the ground by some martyr who thought they could save us all by burning themselves.

For some reason, Eden is different. It was our last vestige of hope and now it's dashed.

"Won't they know you live here?" I ask.

Tony shakes his head.

"No, this ain't our house," Brian says. "Well it is now, but it wasn't before."

Tony is too busy stitching me up. He is on the last half of the deep gash. Only a few more minutes of torture.

"But the picture," I say. "I saw the picture on the mantle. That was you guys."

"When you're running for your life," Tony says, "you grab only your most important possessions. That picture is one of them. We're originally from Mississippi." He squints his eye, his tongue lolling out from the corner of his mouth, and I feel a sharper burst of numbed pain than the ones before. He loops the thread and pulls.

I bite my tongue to avoid screaming like a little girl. The old Jack Jupiter would do that, not this new and improved zombie killer.

"There, all done," Tony says.

I bring my arm back to my side, examining the wound. It hurts just to do that.

"Just need a bandage and it'll heal up in about a week," Tony says.

"Were you a doctor?" Abby asks.

Tony shakes his head. "I sold insurance. Terrible job," he says. "I was close to killing myself every Monday through Friday." He smiles as if he is joking, but somehow I don't think he is. Everyone in the nine-to-five world is basically the same, at least in my experience. They're looking for something to shake up the way things are so they can get that three day weekend or extended vacation. Snowstorm, power outage...plague.

Well, we got it.

"I went to the Mississippi State," Brian says. "Graphic design."

"Really? That's cool," Abby says. She blinks at him like a girl in love. I can already hear the wedding bells. "I was going to go to Ohio State. I'd actually almost be a sophomore now if none of...well, you know."

"This is great and all," I say, kind of annoyed. There's bigger things here to worry about than our old lives. "But my brother is in the clutches of some crazy Army general and we are not there helping him." I get up from the table, the pain from my wound barking as I do so.

"Uh-uh, soldier," Tony says. "Going to Eden now would be suicide, especially hurt."

"Then I'll go alone," I say.

Darlene grabs my bicep. "No," she says. "I'm not going to lose you."

"Darlene, I have to do what I have to do. You understand," I say.

"Let us go with you, Jack," Abby says. "But wait, just

wait. Let us rest and regroup. We'll hit them harder this way."

"They won't see us coming," Darlene says. "We'll go tomorrow."

"They see everything," Tony says.

Brian nods, his eyes fixated on me. All of their eyes are.

I just smile. I will leave them if I have to, gone while they're sleeping, back before they wake up with my brother in hand.

The sun has started to go down, but I am still sweating. I shake, too. With pain, with anger, I don't know. It's a combination of a lot of emotions because I know my brother was there when I needed him the most back in Woodhaven. Forget all about him leaving Mother and I and joining the military. I know why he did it and he's apologized, and he saved Darlene when I couldn't. If it wasn't for him being there that July 4th weekend, she would've been devoured by all the people I grew up hating. So I can't leave him there, not even for a night.

"They won't kill him if that's what you're worried about, Jack," Tony says. "They'll want all the information out of him they can get. Spike takes things extremely...personal."

Herb leans away, back to the cover of the shadows he was in earlier. For a second, I think he is going to run. He doesn't. Just the mention of Spike seems to bring him to his knees.

Still, I voice my opinion on that matter. "I'm not waiting for them to beat him to death. I am going in there and I'm going to kill every last one of those camouflaged bastards." My voice is like a serrated blade sawing through bone.

Tony comes over to me. He puts both hands on my shoulder. There is a brief moment where I think he is going to wring my neck, maybe slap some sense into me.

"Listen to me, Jack," he says, gripping me tighter, "you are not in your right mind. You have experienced great stress. We all have. Norm will be hurt, I won't lie to you, if I saw correctly, he was already shot in the leg. But Spike won't kill him this quick. That, I promise."

I take a deep, steady breath to calm myself, escaping Tony's grasp as I do so. I lean up against a large cabinet that fits as perfectly as a *Tetris* piece into the corner of the kitchen. The fine China dishes inside jingle as I do so. Some dust drifts down from the top. My nose tickles like I'm about to sneeze and I really don't want to cover my mouth with the burning sensation in my arm already revving up to its maximum intensity.

"You're right," I say, already planning my midnight escape.

"Just give it one more night. Let's plan this out first before we go in there guns-a-blazing," Tony says.

I nod. That is the smart choice, the right one. Then I cross the kitchen tile into the living room where the dead TV stares at me, the waning sun going down behind it.

Something moves outside, a shadow, a silhouette. Slow, lumbering movements.

I part the curtains to see glowing yellow eyes. It's just the one at first. One that has strayed from its pack. One that has taken to hunting the night too early while its pack mates wobble from one dead foot to the other, decomposing quicker in the scorching Floridian sun.

Then, I see more. Their yellow eyes glinting with dying light. Each one flicks on like street lamps in an abandoned neighborhood as darkness grows closer.

I blink and they're gone. Maybe I do need some rest.

23

"ARE YOU FEELING ALL RIGHT, JACK?" DARLENE ASKS.

We sit in the upstairs bed, the covers still rumpled from our previous night's stay.

I shake my head. I am not all right. My brother is gone. I am shot. Eden is lost. I am tired and hungry and sad.

"It'll be okay," she says.

Rarely, does Darlene have to console me.

I take a deep breath, close my eyes.

"We'll get Norm back. You're just not ready to start a war," she says. "You saw that man. He held me at gunpoint, Jack. He is crazy. Worse than all the zombies."

"I don't think anyone is ever ready to start a war," I say.

She leans forward and kisses me on the corner of my mouth. “You're right,” she says. “I hate the constant violence. I hate having to be scared all the time.” Her eyes gleam with tears, but she won't let them fall. I see that in her face. She wants to be the strong one here. She wants to be the rock. “I don't want to die. I don't want you to die.”

“Me either,” I say, meaning it.

“We should get to sleep,” she says.

Sleep, that's all we do in bed.

So far since the dead rose, there's not been many times or places to do what engaged couples usually do. In the last few months, I can count how many times we made love undisturbed on one hand. Abby or Norm somehow always interrupted us. Zombies, too. Zombies more than anything. I've come to think of the act as a bad omen.

I lean forward, the wound prickling with a dull sort of pain, and I kiss her full on the mouth. The act is enough to get my blood pumping faster, but I refrain.

A creak outside of the door causes me to turn away from my fiancé's beautiful eyes. Through the cracked door, I see a large, hunched figure.

It's Herb.

“Herb,” I say.

He stops. In a small voice — much too small for a man as big as he is — he says, “Y-Yeah?”

"Come in here, please," I say.

Darlene gives me a look and arches her eyebrow.

I nod: *Don't worry*. It's the kind of mental telepathy only soulmates can have.

"O-Okay," Herb says.

I pat the end of the bed.

"What makes you so special?" I ask him.

He shrugs. "Nothin," he says.

I smile, trying to ease the tension.

"C'mon, Herb, don't be bashful," I say.

"He's a super-genius," Darlene says.

Herb shies away as if he's blushing. "No, I'm not a super genius, I'm just a man."

"Then why does Butch want you back?" I ask.

"I'm really not supposed to say," he says. He swallows hard enough for me to hear the gulp.

"Herb...I'm not the police. I'm not going to arrest you or anything like that."

"I know..." he says, "I'm just not proud of it."

Darlene smiles.

She pats Herb. "We've all done things we're not proud of," she says. "Especially now. It's life. But we get through it, accept the responsibility, and move on. That's exactly what you are doing, isn't it, Herb? You didn't like what they were trying to make you do, so you left. You moved on."

Herb smiles — one of those smiles a man cracks in

the fresh sunlight of a new day, the darkness behind him. “Yeah...I guess you’re right,” he says.

“You don’t have to tell if you don’t want to,” Darlene says. “It’s totally up to you, but we think you could help prepare us for what we are going to face in the next couple of days. As much as I’d like for my fiancé to stay in bed and get rest, he won’t.” She smiles at me and leans closer to Herb. In a loud whisper, she says, “He’s a stubborn little mule.”

Herb bursts out in laughter.

It’s really not that funny, but I find myself laughing with him. The world has been devoid of *real* laughter for too long. All those times I should’ve laughed but have been too depressed have been bubbling inside of me and now they’re boiling over. I can’t help it. Darlene laughs, too.

The laughter eventually fades. Abby and the Richards’s below us must think we’re batshit crazy.

Herb wipes his eyes. “Okay, okay,” he says, in a more serious tone. “I ain’t super smart in all aspects of life. I never learned how to drive a car real good for one thing. Almost fifty years old and I can’t remember what side of the double lines I’m s’posed to be on.” He chuckles. “But I’m good at sums and science stuff. Couldn’t tell you a damn thing about the *peri-odd-ik* table, no — besides oxygen, that stuff we breathe, and carbon, that stuff that makes the soda pop bubble, but I can figure out how to make things mix together good to make medicines and potions, like the witches in those scary movies my aunt Maggie used to take me to when I was a kid. That was September 18th, 1977, last time I saw Auntie Maggie alive. It was a Sunday. She took care of me and Phil when my momma died. She died the year after on August 2nd, 1978. That woulda been... " He brings a finger up to his forehead and squeezes his eyes shut until his face is a mess of wrinkles. "That woulda been a...Wednesday. Yeah, a Wednesday!" He's smiling now, then he shakes his head and waves a hand. "'Cuse me, I'm getting all remember-y."

Darlene pats his large shoulders again. "No, Herb, it's all right."

I nod. Wow. Herb has a gift. One you would miss if you wrote him off as a mentally handicapped man. As I almost did.

"I can do these things real nice," he says. "That's what Spike and Butch tell me. I can help them solve the problem...you know, the dead people." His eyes jam shut again. "Gosh, I hate dead people. They're all... runny and scary." His eyes light up again. "Like those witches in the scary movies my aunt Maggie used to take me to when I was a kid!"

"So what did he have you do?" I ask.

Herb shies away again, goes into that mental cocoon.

"It's all right, Herb," Darlene says.

I asked Tony and Brian, but they didn't know. They'd only seen Herb a handful of times. Matter of fact, they'd only seen Spike a handful of times, too. Butch is the guy who does the dirty work, who takes the blame when things goes wrong. Spike, I presume, is the king of the castle, the one the citizens of Eden bow down to, the one whose feet they kiss. But he's also the mastermind, the evil madman who will burn down a village of uninfected just for a small bottle of aspirin, then that same night, he'll sleep like a baby knowing he cured a couple of headaches. Yeah, I know guys like that. I've written about them all my life, dealt with them in high school — Freddy Huber would bash your brains in after gym class, but he'd be praised for making the game-winning touchdown pass later that same night.

It's a basic fact of life, I'm afraid. There's assholes and the people they shit on.

These are obviously just huge assumptions. I've never met Spike, but it's safe to say any guy who sends out a task force of gunslinging Jugheads is not a stable man.

"I don't know, really," Herb says. "They was having me work with this man. I really liked him. Real smart guy. Said he came from the CDC in Washington and I try to tell him I don't listen to them CDs. Never did. My aunt Maggie left me a record player when she died. It worked before I had to leave home. I miss that record player...I miss my aunt Maggie."

He leans forward, huge hands covering his face, and what comes out of his mouth is nothing close to laughter. It's sobs, deep, rumbling sobs.

Darlene still has her hand on his back, and she looks at him, her eyes bulging. That mental telepathy: *Do something, Jack! Help me!*

Then me responding with a left-hand scratch of my forehead which transitions to me pushing my too-long hair out of my eyes. *What the heck do I do?*

Anything, Jack!

Growing up in Woodhaven, I remember my mom working a double at the diner on my eighth birthday and bringing me a half-eaten piece of apple pie with a burning cigarette plopped in the middle as a candle — so yeah, I'm not the best when it comes to comfort.

Jack, come on!

Herb's sobs ramp up to something rivaling the shifting of tectonic plates.

I put my left hand on his knee, and he jerks at the touch. "It's all right, Herb," I say. "L-Let it out?" I'm looking at Darlene and she rolls her eyes. The motherly instincts come out. I would say all women are gifted with these instincts, but then I'll think of my own mother and know that's not true.

Darlene wraps her arms around Herb. His sobs

subside for the moment. It's so funny seeing my small fiancé up next to him, but it is also sweet. Now I act on instinct, and I join the hug. Herb's sobs stop. He pats me on the back with those big mitts, rattling my bones.

"They-they wanted me to cut one of the dead guys' heads open. They wanted me to cut his brain up," Herb says.

"Why, Herb?"

He rubs his eyes. "I-I don't know." His voice is deep and commanding. No mental telepathy here, it's obvious enough that I'm another few words away from poking the bear.

"Because Spike is crazy," Tony Richards says from the doorway.

It startles me.

"He's crazy, yeah," Darlene says, eyeing Tony, "we already know that."

"Everyone in this world is crazy," I say. It's a sentiment I'd defend with my last dying breath.

"Not the kind of crazy y'all think he is," Tony says. "He's crazier than that."

"Well, putting Butch Hazard in charge of your security is pretty damn crazy, then kidnapping my brother is also pretty damn crazy."

"He wants to control an army," Tony says.

"Hope someone breaks it to him before he gets too far ahead of himself, but there's not enough people left on the face of the earth for an honest-to-God army."

Tony chuckles and shakes his head. "You don't get it, do you?"

I tilt my head. "No?" I say it more like a question.

"Not an army of living people, but an army of the dead."

24

"YOU'VE GOT TO BE KIDDING ME," I SAY, SHAKING MY head.

That *is* crazy.

"No, I ain't," Tony says. "Ask Brian. Hell, ask Herb here if he's up to talking about it." Herb shifts farther away from Tony at the sound of his name. "Butch is crazy, but Spike is crazier."

Someone creaks up the steps. In my fuzzed-brain state, I picture the golden-eyed monsters I thought I saw outside.

A voice drifts toward us.

It's Brian. "So crazy that he needs put down. When Dad was shooting at him, we was so close." He uses his thumb and index finger to showcase just how close. Then he snarls, reminding me of a rabid dog — thin, mangy...and hungry for a kill. "But Butch Hazard deserves worse than a bullet to the brain. I wanna make him suffer like he made me suffer."

Herb starts sobbing again. "Poor Tammy." Blubbering. "I-I-I heard about her." More blubbers. "S-S-S-She died on a Monday. I always hated Mondays."

Tony bows his head. "Yeah, poor Tammy."

"I'm sorry, I don't mean to pry — " I begin. I definitely am, but the curiosity is too great for me to let this one go.

"She was my wife. My pregnant wife. We thought we were safe..." Brian answers, but the stern look on his face, the disgust, the pain, the hurt, doesn't stay long. He screws up his features like a rain cloud swollen with a storm, and he bursts. Sobs, deep, wracking sobs that almost rival Herb's cut through the quiet farmhouse.

Herb gets up from the bed and walks over to Brian. He hugs him, swallows him up in his large embrace. The two sob, first loudly then quietly while Tony Richards bows his head and closes his eyes. I am too tired to cry, but I feel sadness. We have all lost others. Me, I lost my mom and my friends in Woodhaven, I almost lost Darlene, and now I've lost Norm. Abby lost her mom, too — worst, she had to kill her own zombified version of her mom. She's talked of other family, long-distance relatives she's met once or twice in life, but she speaks of them like strangers. The point is, we all lost people, but we are still here and I don't know if that is a gift or a curse sometimes.

Once the crying subsides, Brian starts to talk. "I met Tammy three days after we arrived at Eden. By that time, it still had some of its grace left. Green grass in front of the lawns, flower beds (Mom loved the flower beds), and a sense of security we couldn't find anywhere else. It smelled normal...you know, *alive.* We were all given jobs. Stupid folk labor, really.

"I was one of Eden's landscapers. Tammy would sit out on her assigned shelter's porch, a sun hat on her head, always wearing a frilly, low-cut dress. I don't throw pansy terms around like 'love at first sight' often, but that's exactly what it was." He sighs and looks out the window into the sunlight's last fading rays. "Yeah, Tammy's house was my favorite to 'scape. I'd do my best work over there, and always take way longer than I needed to. Then it got to be that once a week wasn't enough to see her. I'd sneak out past the compound's mandated curfew, crawl into her bedroom window. She lived with a cousin, that was all of her family that survived. It wasn't physical at first. We'd talk and laugh and tell stories of the lives we only lived a few months before, but the way we told 'em made it seem like they were forever ago. Then it got physical, and she got pregnant. I wasn't worried, you know, bringing up a baby in a shitty world like this one. I was ready for it. With Tammy by my side, I could do anything."

Darlene looks at me and smiles. I smile back.

"But sometimes the timing ain't right," Brian continues. "Spike pulled a Hitler among the local government of Eden," he says this while making air quotes with both hands. "And imagine if Hitler never lost World War II...that's what Eden was. No more lawn mowing. Now you're in the yard breaking rocks with a pickaxe, helping build them walls with tools you ain't never heard off. The woman and men were separated, but..." he chokes up again. We are all watching him with dark eyes. He is the center of attention. The electricity is off, but he is in the burning spotlight. "But then Spike wanted more. He wanted to find out why these people came back after they died and how he could use that for his advantage. People were selected for experiments."

What? Experiments?

Darlene has her hand over her open mouth, her brow wrinkling. It's the look she used to get whenever an animal died on screen in a movie or TV show. Or when one of her romance books deviated from the Happy Ever After trope.

"Tammy was one of them. My unborn child was another. Two for the price of one that dickhead Spike got," Brian says.

I ball my hands into fists, ignoring the pain in my arm. *Murderer* runs through my head. *Hate* comes soon after.

"Maybe he didn't know," Darlene says, trying to find a ray of hope in the sad tale.

Tony puts an arm around Brian. "Maybe he did, maybe he didn't. Point is, Butch Hazard knew. Butch Hazard knew everything that went on beyond those walls. Who was humping who, what you ate for dinner three nights ago, who's constipated, and so on. He knew Tammy was pregnant. She hadn't started to show yet, but the doctors in town had already put her on them vitamins for the baby — "

"Prenatal vitamins," Darlene says.

"Right," Tony says, nodding. "Prenatal."

"Butch Hazard ripped her from my arms. He pointed a gun in my face, pistol-whipped me, knocked me out cold," Brian says. "Her screams still echo in my head when it's too quiet. It's always too quiet." His hands are shaking.

Herb is now patting him. "There, there," he says.

Now, the sadness that had settled deep inside of me has caught fire, turning into rage, a boiling rage. Butch Hazard had done the same to me, had ripped someone I loved and cared about from my hands.

"That's terrible," Darlene says. "I'm so sorry."

"Yeah," Brian says.

"That son of a bitch has to pay," I say. I feel a fire in my gut. A great blazing fire of rage. "He doesn't get an easy way out."

"Tomorrow," Tony says. "Until then, sleep. Rest your wound."

There's so much adrenaline pumping through my body, I had forgotten about the bullet graze, and the mere mention of it brings me back to earth, the pain revving up from dull to almost unbearable. Tony is right. I have the luxury of a bed, and my fiancé next to me. I have to take advantage of it while I can.

Besides, Norm is tough. Butch Hazard won't be able to break him as easily as he thinks...at least I hope. And we all know where hope has gotten us so far.

25

I DON'T WAKE TO THE SOUNDS OF JOYOUS STOMPING ON the roof or drunken laughter or clattering dishes, but to the sounds of screams instead. My own demented alarm clock.

The darkness is full, there is no chance the sun will come up anytime soon. It must be three, maybe four o'clock in the morning. I look outside the window.

Hundreds of golden eyes glitter in the yard below me. Maybe I shouldn't say they glitter, that's too cute. These are the eyes of the dead, of the rotting bodies. These are eyes that don't work properly, that can't see anything besides their next victims — food, flesh, brains.

Darlene stirs out of bed. The covers once belonging to some long-dead person rustling. She wears a shirt that shows her belly button and a pair of panties. Any other time, looking over my shoulder at her as she glides over to me, I'd be in awe of her beauty.

Right now, though, all I can think about is getting a weapon.

They seem to come from everywhere. Zombie after zombie after zombie.

"Oh my God, Jack," Darlene says. "Am I still asleep?"

I shake my head. I wish we were. I wish this was all a dream.

"Let's go! Battle stations, people!" Tony hisses from the darkness outside of the door. "They're coming and there's a helluva lot of them."

"Maybe we should let them pass," Darlene says. Her voice is hopeful, but she knows as well as I know these things never just 'pass.' They can smell food a mile away, it seems. I grab Darlene's hands. They are cold, clammy, and shaking. "Darlene," I say, "listen to me. There's a lot of them and not many of us."

"Jack — "

"No," I say. "You can't cute your way out of this. As much as I hate to admit it, this is the world we live in. And I love you, you know I love you. So much. I would be lost without you. I almost went crazy thinking about you walking around in Woodhaven like one of those... those *things*."

"Jack, I'm...I can't," she says.

"You have to."

Brian steps in, Abby on his side. They have just woken up and part of me thinks they might've just woken up in the same bed. It's none of my business, though. *Definitely* not the time.

"What's going on?" Brian asks.

"A horde," I say as I walk over to the chair my pants are draped over. As I'm pulling them up, I give Darlene a look, one that says no more messing around, no more being afraid. It's time to step up.

That includes me. I am not going to lose another one of my family members.

"Wake up Herb and get ready," I say.

"I think he's already up," Abby says.

I tilt my head at her. "Wait, what? That wasn't you screaming?"

She rolls her eyes. "Jack, do I ever scream like that?"

I weigh that statement for a moment. No. Abby is one of the toughest gals I know.

"So, yeah, Herb is up," I say.

"Why don't we just leave?" Darlene asks. "Get in the car and leave!"

"We won't make it out there," I say. "We can't wade through a sea of zombies, you know that, Darlene. If it was just a few of them, yeah, I'd say we get out there and blow their brains out. But it's not."

"Is it really that much?" Brian asks, still sounding half-asleep.

I point to the window where the snarls of the dead drift up to us like a thick smoke. He walks over. "Holy shit," he says. "It's almost as bad as what we saw in Atlanta."

Darlene goes rigid next to me.

I give Brian a look, one of those *Come on, man, really?* looks.

He catches the glare and says, "Not bad. We can wipe them out. Easy." But his voice is about as convincing as you'd think. Darlene doesn't relax. I shepherd her out of the room and into the hallway.

Tony has his silenced pistol in hand, and his sniper rifle draped over his back at the foot of the stairs.

He is not surprised to see us. His eyes are distant. He is already focused on the impending battle.

I have Norm's Magnum and Abby has the Midnight Special. Darlene has the Glock, though she will only use it if she absolutely has to.

I wish we had something better. An AR15, maybe... oh, well, I've fought with worse.

Tony glances at Darlene coming down the steps with the Glock. "Careful with that thing," he says.

She looks back at him with a face that says, *Really, man?* It's a pure look of disgust, the same look she gave a carny in charge of the milk bottle game at the Cook County Fair after he mocked her. *You throw like a girl!* It was before she clobbered him in the bridge of the nose with a fastball that would've made Roger Clemons envious.

She is a very capable woman, if she puts the fear to the back of her mind.

"I know how to shoot a gun," she says. "I'm not stupid."

"Good," Tony says.

Abby, Brian, and Herb come down the steps after her. Herb is saying something to himself over and over again. A silent prayer, I think.

Creaking from beyond the front door shuts him up, shuts us all up. We hardly even breathe. Boy, it never gets old, does it? No matter how many times I hear those terrible death rattles, the sounds of lungs no longer taking in air, of the oxygen sitting in their throats, I will never get used to it.

"Start barricading," Tony says.

Abby and I exchange a glance. The darkness is almost total and we barely can see the whites of our eyes let alone the guns in our hands, but we both know barricading is a fool's game. We both know this from experience. You can't keep the zombies out. The most you can do is fight or give up, and we damn sure aren't giving up.

Tony tiptoes around the corner into the living room, Brian at his heel. They make way too much noise as they try to drag something out. I know this because the creaking increases from outside, as if the zombie out there ahead of all its friends is rocking back and forth in excitement. An excited puppy trying to find a way into the overflowing garbage can.

"They ain't gonna get in, are they?" Herb asks me.

"No," I say. "We won't let them in. We won't let them hurt you." But if I really believed that I wouldn't be shaking.

"Promise?" he asks.

"Yes, pinky promise."

Herb smiles as his massive pinky engulfs mine.

"Now go hide," I say, then turn and grab Darlene. "You ready?" I ask her.

She doesn't answer immediately. There's a long pause while more snarls creep through the cracks in the door. "Yes," she says. "But only because you got *some* rest, and because it gets us closer to Norm."

I smile at that.

Family is family.

I don't have to ask Abby if she's ready. She's already holding her gun, arms tensed, body in battle-ready position. She, like me, is a zombie slaying professional. We know what is to come. We know no barricade or walls can separate us from the dead.

With Herb behind us, chattering, sticking to the shadows, we move toward Brian and Tony. I am in the lead, Darlene behind me and Abby behind her, almost how we were in Woodhaven as I led them out of the inferno and into Norm's Jeep.

But this is somehow different. I get a bad feeling about this, like somehow this is just the beginning of the storm and not the end like it was back in my old hometown.

The two get a barricade up fast. They've not only stacked the couches, but they've also stacked a loveseat, a recliner. Tony is working on covering the windows as the glass breaks. It comes from the recreation room. There is a large pool table in the middle, the green felt covered in dust and cobwebs. Pool sticks line the wood-paneled walls, and mounted on these walls are the victims of hunter's game: deers and bears and some fish.

The window that has broken is one of two long panes of glass, green curtains bunched up on either side. Limbs poke through as does faint moonlight, painting the rotten skin in a pearl-like glow. Broken glass rips down the side of an arm. No blood spills from the wound. Seeing it causes my own blood to freeze up in my veins. I feel Darlene going rigid against me.

Whatever blood is in these zombies has since been boiled out of them by the scorching Floridian sunshine. I see a gleam of white bone. Then I see a face. Long, matted hair frames this face. One eye glows bright yellow, the other is dimmer, almost cataract. I will never get used to seeing this, I will never fully get rid of the fear that comes with staring down a zombie. One that is especially close and ready to eat you.

So I aim the Magnum straight ahead, and squeeze the trigger.

That helps a little.

26

THE ZOMBIE'S FACE EXPLODES IN A MESS OF PINK AND gray brains. The flash from the muzzle lights this up in excruciating horror.

The fear is back. Everything I've ever seen in a horror movie or imagined while reading or writing a book goes out the window.

This is real.

This is terrifying.

Once the shot's echo fades in my head, I hear the faint shrieks and squeals from Darlene.

"Steady," I tell her. "Steady." But not even my voice is steady. A deaf person could hear that.

At this same time, the couch and love seat start to shift. There's more on the front porch now. I know from experience, they can push a door open with enough force. It's only a matter of time.

"Other side," I shout to Brian.

"Window's too far up," he says over the snarls. "They won't be able to — "

"Brian, listen to him!" Abby says.

"If there's enough, they'll find a way in," I say. I don't say that we have to find a way out.

Two more make their way in through the window. And two more shots sound. One from me, and one from Abby. When I turn to her, my ears ringing, she is still looking at Brian, the gun raised in her hand.

"Brian, go!" I yell. "Before even more get in."

Tony has his back to the barricade on the front door. Above us, over all the racket, the moans and groans, the breaking glass, I hear Herb's soft and deep cries.

Don't worry, big guy, we are going to get out of this. Just hold on.

Tony lurches forward. The creak of the door's hinges come first, then the leaning of the couch and the loveseat. The door is locked, but I see the wood swell outward.

The wood starts to splinter. Each crack brings a gasp up from Darlene's throat, and a skitter in my heartbeat.

As I aim down the Magnum, seeing the sight jitter in sync with my shaking hands, I wonder if it's my fate knocking on the front door.

27

Darlene looks to me, her big, puppy dog eyes — now even bigger on her gaunt face. They all look at me. I am their leader and they want to know what we should do.

The door is broken open now, and from the wound spills the dead. The moon seems brighter. The room has grown hotter. I smell earth and decay and rain in the air.

There is only one thing we can do, and that's fight.

"Jack?" Darlene says. "Where are they coming from?"

I *have* to be strong for this woman who has stolen my heart.

"Doesn't matter," I say. "We are gonna kill them all."

She grips my hand, her touch like a buzz of

electricity both jolting me out of my hopelessness and spurring me forward.

Fight. We have to fight.

"Tony, outta the way!" I shout. And with a slight shove, I guide Darlene toward the steps. "Go get Herb. Abby and Brian, watch our flanks!"

Abby and Brian scurry across the hallway. Abby pauses and her gun cracks. I don't see the zombie she's shot, but I hear its lifeless corpse thumping the carpet.

Darlene stands on the steps to the second floor, looking at me differently than before. With a look of admiration, of pride.

I smile the slightest bit, an alien emotion in a time like this, but one I can't help but portray. "Go get Herb, Darlene. We're getting out of here."

She nods, turns and runs up the stairs.

"She's right. Never seen so many out here. Something is off," Tony says.

Damn right. It's been off for half a year.

Tony has his pistol, and he is not hesitant about pulling the trigger.

My own weapon shudders in my hands. I feel the power surging through my body.

One zombie's head explodes, then another, and another.

With our combined shooting, the door completely blows off.

The shots stop, and vibration runs through my

hands and forearms. My own wound burns, but I hardly notice it over the adrenaline pumping through my body. The little bit of sleep I got definitely helps.

Behind us, Abby's gun blasts in intermittent bursts. Brian's does, too.

There is a pile of dead zombies laying over the couch, which is also riddled with holes. Stuffing floats in the air like summer snow. I smell death, not even the smell of gunpowder can drown that out. There is dark blood splashed on the walls of the earth and mud-color wallpaper. A trail of guts and brains on the ceiling, drops swelling then falling. A pool of red grows larger and larger by the second, not even the hallway runner can absorb all of it.

Inside of my head, I hear this terrible *eeeeEeeeee* noise that I don't think will leave me for an hour, hell, maybe even a day. My eardrums were not ready for tonight.

Tony says something to me, but his voice is distant and swimmy. I read his lips, basically, and my brain fills in the rest with a cheap imitation of his gruff voice.

"The path is cleared, let's get the fuck out of here," he is saying.

I nod.

"Darlene! Come on!" I shout, or at least I think I shout. Right now, the feeling I'm stuck with is having earbuds in with the volume all the way up while trying to carry on a normal conversation.

Through the hole in the wall, more zombies shamble from the dead grass and crop field. I estimate we have about two minutes before another swarm of them hits the porch.

"The Dodge," Tony says.

His voice comes to me in waves. Sometimes muted, sometimes really loud. I'm like a frayed A/V cable.

I shake my head. "No, we attack Eden now," I say. There's too much adrenaline going through my body to lay low.

"Jack," Tony starts to say, but is cut off by Herb's heavy footsteps banging the steps.

Herb has his hands over his eyes, his head slouched. Darlene is behind him, guiding his large torso with her small hand.

"Jack, we are not ready," Tony says. "We are outnumbered, outgunned, injured..." He is looking at me like the teacher who just caught you cheating on a big math test. That look of accusation and betrayal.

"I am ready. I am going. You and Brian can do whatever you want. You don't owe us anything."

"I'm in," Brian says. "After what Butch did to my Tammy, I'd go even if the only weapon I had was a fork." I imagine the adrenaline is pumping through him, too.

Herb peeks out from beneath his hands and nods his head. "I don't wanna go back, but I will for you,

Jack. You protected me from them now I'll protect you."

The way he speaks makes me want to cry. Why anyone would do anything for Jack Jupiter is beyond me. So I smile, hoping no one sees the tears brimming in my eyes, and pat him on the back.

Abby is smiling as she says, "You already know I'm in…even if Norm is an asshole. Maybe they knocked some sense into him, and I want to live to see that."

I chuckle. "Doubt it. He's stubborn."

Darlene says, "I go wherever you go, Jack Jupiter."

Then everyone looks at Tony. His long beard sways as he shakes his head. He sighs, turns toward the bullet-blown hole in the wall and strokes his beard. "Fine," he says. "Staying here won't do me no good."

A smile breaks across my face.

Humanity may be slowly dying, evaporating from the face of the earth, but there's humanity here, right now, in this shitty farmhouse.

The dead don't care for humanity. They still come.

Small triumphs are never as cut and dry as they are in the movies.

I am tired, my wound hurts, I am missing my brother, and I am in a strange place surrounded by zombies. Yet, somehow, I am all right. I am with my family.

So I lead the way to the outside, through the hole Tony and I made with our guns, and I think to myself that I am Johnny Deadslayer on a mission to save his captured brother from beyond enemy lines.

But as I step out onto the porch, carefully so as not to step in brains or guts, I am bathed in bright, blinding headlights.

Butch Hazard is on the loudspeaker again, his voice grating and haunting, "Sometimes life is a bitch," he says.

28

THE TRUCK IS THE CAUSE OF THE BRIGHT, WHITE headlights. I am shielding my eyes, the pistol still in hand, and Darlene cowering behind me. But there is more than the trucks. I see four red lights hovering in the distance like glowing, red eyes. I think of some great beast lurking in the shadows. They are the trailers of semi-trucks, parked a ways off the road. One of the trailers is open. Zombies stream out from inside. *Son of a bitch,* I think. *That son of a bitch flushed us out with zombies* —

That thought is banished once I hear the steady *beep-beep-beep,* and those red eyes get closer. It's a sound I haven't heard in the better part of a year, a sound I didn't know I missed until hearing it just now. The other trailer backs up through the field.

A few of the dead scramble. Just a few. We could

take them. The bulk of the zombies are piled up behind us.

"Welcome to Hell," Butch Hazard says.

Then, as if on cue, a flame lights up in his hands, so does the hands of his soldiers — and he made sure to bring more this time, their guns trained on us. I notice his shoulder is patched as is the bite mark on his hand.

Butch tosses the flaming whatever at the house behind us. Glass shatters as what he throws meets the siding. Fire licks up the side.

"Fire!" he yells to his soldiers.

I involuntarily clench up as I step totally in front of Darlene, Abby, Herb and the Richards.

"Excuse the pun," Butch says as more fire engulfs the house. The back of my head feels singed. I am sweating. My heart is racing. We have no choice but to step forward.

A zombie shambles toward us, orange light glinting off of its yellow eyes. Tony raises his gun to put it down, but a burst of shots rips from one of the soldier's weapons. Bullets thump the soft earth just inches away from Tony's feet, sending a spray of dirt and grass in every direction.

"Nope," Butch says. "No weapons. Put 'em down!"

Darlene is shaking behind me. I wish I could hold her and tell her it's all going to be okay, but I can't because I don't know if that will be the case. Reluctantly, one by one, we drop our weapons.

Brian doesn't throw the silenced pistol out in front of him. "You bastard!" he yells, then he takes off running.

Tony makes a grab at him but misses.

In the glow of the firelight, Butch's harsh face raises into a smile. "Well, would you look at that," he says.

The soldiers's guns crack, shooting at Brian's feet as he rushes forward. But he's not scared. He keeps running.

"Brian!" Tony yells, and goes after him.

As if there is an invisible wall, Brian stops about ten feet in front of Butch. I can do nothing but sit here and burn.

The dead bushes are on fire, now. Heat radiates off of them in waves. Herb squirms behind me. He wants to run. I can practically feel the springs in his large legs readying themselves for a mad dash to freedom. I turn around and put my hand on his forearm. His eyes are wide and he looks at me like I'm a zombie, not a friend. I shake my head.

He closes his eyes tight. A drop of sweat or maybe a tear rolls down his cheek.

"Slowly," I say. "We'll walk slowly, our hands up." I feel like I'm being forced to walk the plank on some pirate ship, the fall below is the field in front of me. Otherwise known as death.

"We can't just leave them," Abby says. "Not Brian."

Her mouth is a thin, bloodless line on her face. She wears a dazed, traumatic look.

"I know," I say. But as if no one else notices the house is on fire, I point to the side where the flames have burned the bushes to a pile of ash and are now working their way up the porch guardrail. "We have to get away from the house before it collapses."

I lead the way, creeping down the porch steps, which are already dancing with small flames.

"You remember me?" Brian shouts at Butch. "Do you fuckin remember me?" He has the pistol trained on Butch's head. But Butch doesn't seem to notice, or care. He looks tired, fed up.

He blinks slowly then turns his head, sighing. I am close enough to hear his voice without the megaphone. He squints at Brian. "No, kid, I don't remember you."

"You took my Tammy," Brian says, his voice choking up. "You took her from me and she was pregnant."

Butch arches an eyebrow.

Tony is on Brian's side. He grabs his arm, tries to pull him away from the truck with its blinding lights and army of assault rifle toting soldiers. "Brian," he says. "Let's — "

"Ring any bells, soldiers?" Butch asks, leaning backward.

A mustached man, wearing the familiar camouflaged outfit as the ones in Sharon answers.

"Yeah, boss," the man answers. "The blonde. Remember? The doc said the kid would've made it — "

"Oh, yeah!" Butch says. He starts laughing. Great, belly-shaking laughs. The kind of laughs you'd hear Santa Claus belting out on Christmas. Except, Butch isn't an old and jolly fat man. He's a stern-faced killer. The laughter escaping his throat is about as alien as Darlene with a gun. "Yeah, I remember her. She was a pretty young thing. If she wasn't pregnant, I might've kept her for myself."

Brian lunges, but now Tony has both hands on him, holding him back.

Where we are standing, we see this perfectly. For Abby, maybe too perfectly. She lunges too, but I grab her before she can do anything stupid. The center of attention might be on Butch Hazard and Brian, but the soldiers aren't dumb. Half of them have their weapons trained on us. Where the large semi-trucks are, there's more soldiers with their guns raised.

"You've all been summoned to Eden," Butch says. "So cool it, kid. Drop the gun and quit being an idiot."

"Fuck Eden," I shout. If I'm going to die, it's going to be on my own terms.

"Yeah, fuck Eden," Brian echoes.

Butch laughs, looking at me. "Just like your brother," he says. "You know, he's still alive...barely. He held tough for a while before he gave this place up. Only lost a few teeth. Maybe has a ruptured spleen. I don't know, really, we don't let the doctor utilize his talents on garbage."

It's like a stab straight to my heart. I suspected torture, but I had no confirmation. My body starts to shake. I'm a rocket on the launchpad. The fire is burning through me. "I swear to God if you hurt — " I begin, but Brian cuts me off.

"This ain't about them," he says, making a move at Butch, breaking free from his father's grip. But Butch is there, he wraps both hands around Brian's neck and both of their faces start to turn red.

Butch Hazard is a man of war. He's planned this out. No doubt Norm had given him all the details in order to spare his fingers. I don't blame my older brother for this, either. I would've cracked much earlier than he did. Thinking of Norm all bloodied and begging for mercy causes me to grit my teeth.

"That was my wife," Brian says. I can barely hear him.

"Not anymore, kid. She's in one of those dead bastard's rotten intestinal tracts now."

Brian bucks, kicking his legs out, beating at Butch's hands.

No luck.

Butch just smiles, but his eyes are harsh. Black onyx set in an aging face. His left hand goes to the knife on his belt, and he pulls it free. I think he's going to cut Brian's throat right here on the spot. But he doesn't. He lets go of Brian, the gun dropping from his hand, and then he puts the blade, handle first, into Brian's fist. "You're welcome to try and find her chewed up remains," he says.

"You son of a bit — " Brian says, but his voice is drowned out by thunder.

I think, for a moment, as this registers in my head, that a storm has broken out above us. I remember smelling rain and the clouds seemed heavy, ready to burst.

But lightning does not come from eye level. It comes from above. And this lightning did not come from high in the sky. It came from Butch Hazard's Desert Eagle. He moved so fast I barely saw him.

I do see the rain, though. Not water, but blood. A thick curtain of it suspended in animation. Heavy, red, terrifying.

My head hums with the shot.

The zombies' strained groans and cries for food are amplified. Yet, some of them seem muffled. In the burst of light, I see smiles on the faces of the soldiers. People who signed up to see exactly this.

Behind me, Abby screams.

I can't believe this...any of it.

Then, as if on cue, Brian spins around. I don't know if it is because of the force of the bullet or because this is God's cruel way of proving to me that what I hear and see is real, but Brian looks at me with one good eye. His other eye is missing. Gone, nothing but a gristly black void. A river of blood flows from a fist-sized hole in his forehead. Despite all of this, Brian looks calm, as if none of this has happened at all. As if I cannot see his exposed brains, pulsing pink in the dying moonlight.

Tony cries out, reaches for his son who is falling over. This plays in front of me in slow motion as moments of tragedy often do. I want to reach for him, I want to grab Brian and stop him from hitting the dirt. Because once he hits the dirt, then it's all but final.

I can't move.

And Brian hits the dirt.

Butch laughs, and like an old Western black hat, he brings the gun up to his mouth and blows the smoke away.

Brian is dead.

29

"Don't look so sad, guys," Butch says. "Now, he can go see his wife in hell. She was a dead fuck, anyway." He laughs again. My vision is blacking out. The veins in my eyes feel like they are bulging. It's taking everything inside of me not to run over and try to kill this bastard.

Tony holds Brian in his arms, blood gushes from the wound.

"You monster," Abby says quietly from my side.

Orange light seems to stretch high over our heads, casting this macabre scene in a warm glow. Beams and siding crackle under the wrath of the fire. I hear something crumble, glass shatter from the tremendous heat.

"You bastard!" Abby screams.

She takes off from her spot. This doesn't play in

slow motion. She is lightning quick, too fast for either me or Darlene to grab her.

Butch's laughter dies. He looks at Abby rushing over at him as if he can't believe his eyes. She stops short once the soldiers' guns raise on her. It must be nice to have your own private cavalry.

"Abby," Darlene says. "Don't!"

Butch stands with his hands on his hips. He's much taller than Abby, looking down at her. She swings at him, at his face, I'm assuming, but misses. Instead, she hits his chest.

Butch doesn't even flinch.

"Oh, how cute," he says as she hits him again.

I am still frozen to the spot. I want to stop this before he can blow her head off, too.

Abby swings again, catching the bottom of Butch's jaw. The playful look of amusement vanishes.

She swings again, and he grabs her fist. Abby cries out in pain as he twists. She crumbles to the ground and Butch stomps a boot down on her, pinning her to the dirt. She lays halfway in a pool of Brian's blood. She's screaming.

That's it. The rage wins out, and I'm rushing across the grass, the fire burning behind and *inside* of me.

Guns come up in my direction, so many guns. Flames glint off the dark metal of their barrels. All these soldiers have murder in their eyes. That sharp look of recklessness, of hope. Maybe they'll get to kill something that's not already dead and moving around like a drunken three-legged dog.

"Leave her out of this," I say. I stand straight up. My mother always told me to stand up straight. People respect someone who stands up straight. That sentiment was echoed the more time I spent with Norm, except he didn't want anyone's respect, he wanted their fear, and that's what I want. I want Butch Hazard to fear me.

That doesn't seem to be the case. He stands straight up, too. Perhaps even more straight than myself.

I think we are going to fight again. A fist fight to end all fist fights. One that I will win.

That's not the case.

Butch snorts laughter, looking at us as if we are not worth his time. He turns to his soldiers and says, "Round 'em up. Put 'em in the trucks. I'm sick of this bullshit. One wrong move and you shoot them in the foot."

I stand helplessly as twenty soldiers with AR15s swarm us.

We are roughly handcuffed, except for Herb. He is too big for regular handcuffs. One man with war paint under his eyes holds him at gunpoint. "Put your hands out. Move the slightest bit and you lose a nut, my big friend. They want you alive, but they don't need you with a full sack."

Herb obeys. They put these big shackles around

his wrists. A chain dangles from these wrist cuffs and I realize, because the firelight glints off the rest of the silver, there are two other unoccupied cuffs for his ankles. They clasp those around him, too, and he looks like Florida's biggest escaped convict. The whole time he sniffles and tries to hold down his sobs with not much luck. Seeing him like that breaks my heart.

Then, out of the corner of my eye, I see the female soldier picking Darlene up.

"Don't you fucking hurt her," I say, my heart breaking even more.

Something rushes up on my other side.

There's a crack, a vibration through my cheekbone, and I realize it's a fist — Butch Hazard's fist. I stumble and fall over on my knees. "No talking to my troops, Jack." He hunches down to look into my eyes. "I won't hold back next punch. If she wants to hurt your girl, she will."

Then he's back up, ripping me up with him, spinning his finger in the air as if making a tornado.

The back half of the house collapses, leaving the living room area with it's blackened chimney jutting up like a dead finger. The siding has since curled off, the porch nothing but soot. I hear the splat of a zombie being crushed under the weight of the fallen walls. Sparks shoot up into the air. I am reminded of Woodhaven.

Then, with a jerk, I am pulled away from the zombies and the ruined farmhouse.

Darlene is, too. We look at each other. Both of our faces are bloodied, me more so.

Somehow, through all the blood and pain and unknown, I smile at her. She smiles back. Right now, I am not Johnny Deadslayer.

30

We are herded to the semi trucks like cattle. If I slow down the slightest bit, I get a boot in the ass. It is not a long walk, but the pain throughout my body makes it feel like one. I am in the lead. Herb is last, and he is flanked by two soldiers as well as led by two others.

The air tastes smoky. My lungs convulse as if I am about to cough, but I know coughing will only make the pain worse, so I don't.

As we approach the semi trucks, the sounds from within them get louder while the sounds of the destruction and chaos are forced to the back of my mind. Behind this thin sheet of metal door are the groans of a hundred zombies. I would recognize those grunts from anywhere.

One of the soldiers throws the door up, the metal

rattling up the track. I jerk backward, running into Butch Hazard's puffed up chest. A burst of pain goes through my midsection as the ribs that were once cracked and healed wrong are bumped again, reminding me to never trust my brother's analysis. But that is the least of my worries. A hand, the flesh hanging off the finger bones like a ripped glove, makes a swipe at my head. Teeth and a dead face with those glowing, yellow eyes are pressed up against a bar. The jaw works. A smell like road kill escapes the open maw of this monster. More zombies take notice and start pummeling into the lead zombie, smashing its face against the cage. I am reminded of an old Play-Doh set I had as a kid, one where you put a ball of the putty in between this masher and pushed with all your might and made Play-Doh spaghetti. Except, this is not so fond. The soft flesh of the zombie's head squishes through the bars. The cranium makes a popping sound then a hiss as dark goo escapes the crack. It falls, its arms still outstretched as it is eventually lost to the shadows and dark, ratty clothing of the other zombies using him as a stepladder.

"First class ride for you assholes," Butch says.

Then his gun presses into my back and I'm forced to crawl up the few steps that lead into the semi's trailer.

The semi is spacious at first glance, but once you step inside and you feel the death pressing up against you, it gets claustrophobic real quick with the cages on both sides. I walk down the aisle between them. It's wide enough for two men to stand side by side, but that would be pushing it. The zombies growl and utter that stupid death rattle. They reach out for me.

"Now you," Butch says.

One of the soldiers throws Tony forward, and it's like throwing an ice cube across a frozen lake. He has no will to stop. He thumps into the steps and falls over, his face coming dangerously close to the stomped zombie who now not only smells like road kill but looks like it, too.

Butch grabs him by the back of the neck. "Want to die, old man?"

Tony doesn't answer.

"Leave him alone, you piece of shit," I say.

Butch looks up at me, a silver gleam in his black eyes. "Or what?"

I don't answer, just stare him down. Now's not the time. Butch Hazard will get his, I'm sure of it, but I won't get to see this if I'm zombie food.

"That's what I thought," he says. He grips Tony harder and pulls him closer. "Answer the question, Richards. Do you want to die?"

Tony still doesn't answer. The way he looks, he might as well be dead — bloody clothes, dirt streaking his face, sweat plastering his hair to his forehead, slicking his beard.

"Yeah, old man, you do. But I'm not gonna give you your wish. You're gonna have to suffer for now."

How nice of Butch Hazard. Fucking prick.

With a shove, Tony goes over the steps and into the aisle where I'm standing, about a foot or so from my feet. Like me, his hands are cuffed behind him so he can't brace the fall with anything but his face and I can't catch him.

The growls of the zombies pick up. They are like hungry dogs locked in a kennel. The noise is enough to make you want to dig your eardrums out with a blade. I bend down to Tony, my knees popping with the motion, my ribs shrieking in agonizing pain. "Come on," I say. He barely moves, but he does move. So he's not dead, that's a good sign.

A hand grasps him around his ankle, the fingernails caked with old blood and dirt. I move fast, faster than my wounds should let me, and I kick the hand at the wrist. It snaps against the bar with a sickening crack. Think dry wood breaking over someone's knee. That kind of crack. But the zombie knows no pain. It knows nothing besides food and making horrible, terrifying guttural sounds. It continues to wiggle its broken arm out at Tony. The others are not as close, and this one can't really do much with a dangling wrist.

"Admirable," Butch says. "But we got a long ride

ahead of us. I'd save that energy for when it really matters, friend." He smiles.

This exchange — but most likely the sound of the breaking bones — snaps Tony out of his fugue state. He scrambles up, eyes the zombies all around him, then looks at me. His expression is one of gratitude and I nod in return.

"Put the two bitches in the other trailer," Butch says.

"Watch your fucking mouth!" I yell at him.

Butch ignores the remark. "Put Herb in with me," he continues. "He's gonna get a *long* talking to. Maybe Spike will put him in the pits after I'm done with him."

Some of the soldiers laugh as if they're all in on some joke. Then one of them says, "Yes, sir!," and grabs the handle of the door and begins to pull it down. In the distance, a shot goes off. Just one burst. I see the lightning bolt of gunfire and the exploding head of a zombie that has strayed too far from the fire.

"Wait!" I yell, my voice raspy and grating. The shout causes a spike in my blood pressure, which sets the wounds all over my body ablaze. "Don't split us up, please." I'm reduced to this, to begging.

Butch still wears the same smile. "Just following orders, Jack. Before you know it, we'll all be eating dinner together in Eden. Like a fucking fairy tale."

Darlene looks at me. There is no worry on her face, only determination. And the door closes.

31

There is no light inside of the trailer. No airflow, either, besides the little bit of hot wind that slips through the cracks of the metal — and it is not much. I stand sideways in the aisle, Tony next to me, matching my same position. Each bump we go over sends us to the bars, where the faintly glowing eyes of the zombies wait for us.

So far, we are okay.

"I'm sorry," I say to Tony.

I feel like this is my fault, I feel like if I would've stayed the course, none of this would've happened.

"Don't be," he says. "Brian was my boy, but he's gone now. Nothing I can do. I am old enough to have loved and lost before. It hurts, yes. Life goes on."

We have to talk loud over the rumble of the engine,

the constant jangling of the bars, and the moans of the zombies.

"Besides, It's not your fault. Ain't no one's fault. I loved my son, don't get me wrong." He sniffles. I can't tell if he's crying and I'm glad for that. If I saw the tough, old Tony Richards cry, this crazy-looking man who keeps corpses in his basement and who can shoot an ant's balls off from five-hundred yards away, I'd start crying myself. And Johnny Deadslayer would never cry, so neither does Jack Jupiter by default.

"If we would've never come to the farmhouse — " I begin to say.

"But you did. That's the way things happened. That's the way life is. We can't change it. We have no control. Butch Hazard is a sick son of a bitch and he will get his, that I'm sure, Jack. Whether it's by me or you or these damn monsters or a freak lightning bolt, he'll get it. I take comfort in knowing that."

Me, too. Tony is right. Butch is going to get his, I'll make sure of it.

The truck lurches, and we are launched to the left. I don't resist, I go with the motion, kicking my leg out and finding purchase against one of the metal bars. Tony does the same. A little less gracefully, but I don't hear any chomps or screams, so he's all right.

"Eden ain't what it used to be, Jack. I told you that once before."

"I know, if I would've listened and gone somewhere else — "

"You'd never be in this mess," Tony says. "Brian would still be alive, yada yada yada. That's bullshit. Butch and his gang would've found you or you would've found Herb and they would've found you then. It was meant to be this way because it happened this way."

"I — " Another bump, this one sends the floor out from beneath me. I land with a jerk and stumble to the left. A zombie is there to greet me, smashing its face against the bars. This one is a girl with hair the color of old bones. I only know this because, like moonlight, it seems to glow in the darkness. I am quick to back away and regain my footing.

"You okay, Tony?" I ask.

"Just peachy," he answers. "Well, I'd had enough standing for the day. Frankly, I don't feel very energetic. I'm getting up there in age. Before you know it, Jack, it's just gone. You lose it. So I'm gonna sit down, put my back up against the door..." I hear his bones cracking, somehow louder than the constant drone of the truck's engine, as he sits, "And maybe take a nap." A zombie screeches. "Aw, shut the hell up, you devil!" The zombie does, in fact, they all do. It's eerie.

Goosebumps prickle up my skin, but I can't complain. The momentary quiet is nice, but with it comes the worry and fear. Darlene is essentially by herself. Abby is beaten and broken, of no help to my fiancé. Herb is in the cabin, riding first class with Butch Hazard. I have no idea where my brother is, and I am suffering from multiple injuries, trapped in a trailer with about a hundred creatures that crave human flesh and guts.

Things are not looking good.

Like a kid during a long car ride, I say, "Tony, are we there yet?"

"We got a ways, cowboy. Rest up while you can and make sure you bring your six-shooter."

"What?" I ask, but he never answers me. I chalk it up to trauma. When people go through messed up times, they don't stay right in the head. Understandable. But the calmness in his voice scares me, too. He speaks like a man who has never suffered at all in his life. I know that's not true. Tony Richards has suffered. He is suffering now.

Hell, in this dead, piece of shit world, we all suffer.

32

I HAVE JUST GARNERED UP THE COURAGE TO SIT DOWN ON the other side of the trailer, my back against the side closest to the front of the semi. Tony snores opposite of me, and the zombies make no noise. How any of this is possible is beyond me. But I'll take it.

I start to drift off moments later. This is probably not the smartest thing I have ever done, but my body is in command now. Bye, bye, brain.

The last image I see in my head before the blackness takes over is of Darlene. She is dressed in a white gown. I am not a man who appreciates the girly things in life — fashion, wedding dresses, make up, and so on — but this dress is beautiful. It is made for Darlene. She smiles the slightest bit beneath a veil. Her eyes glow bright in the dim light surrounding us. I am moving closer. My hands go out in front of me. I realize I'm wearing long-sleeves. I look down, see my reflection in the polished, dark shoes on my feet. I am wearing a tuxedo. Candles dance lazily behind Darlene. I am not walking as much as I am floating. I smell flowers and people, the scents of many of them crowded into a room — perfume, mint chewing gum, coffee-breath. I look to my left and see we are in a church with a high-vaulted ceiling. All the pews are full. People wear their Sunday's finest, packed shoulder to shoulder. People I don't recognize at first, but when I squint my eyes and scan the front row, I see my mother. She is how I remember her, not how I last saw her. My brother is there, too, as his eighteen-year-old self. Abby, Kevin, James, Sheriff Doaks behind him.

"Good job, little brother," Norm says to me, and he smiles.

I lean closer, feeling my eyes getting wider, but not seeing clearly. From Norm's mouth spills a wave of black sludge. I scream. No sound comes out. I want to move, but I am nailed to the floor.

This is when the lights go out and my heart drops to my knees. I smell smoke, but something else overpowers it. The smell of rotting corpses.

The lights kick back on. Everyone in the crowd is different. Their Sunday finest has changed into their burial clothes, and they've been buried a long time. Dirt cascades off their shoulders in thin clouds as they stand up. Worms wiggle from their eye sockets. Some of them have no lips, their faces smiling forever.

My mother is opened in the middle. She has not rotted yet. Her organs hang out of her like candy in a half-busted piñata. A chunk of her nose is gone, in the flesh are little teeth marks — I can't tell if they are from a human or from some animal like the sheriff has told me *(When?) (How?) (Help).*

I try to scream again. Nothing.

Rustling of papers behind me. I turn to look. It is the same priest who spoke when I buried Mother. He is flipping through his Bible. It is moldy and dank. Like him. Maggots squirm in his dirty eyebrows. He smells like rotten milk and sweetness. I want to throw up.

"Ah, yes, here we are," he says, and he smiles. The folds of his flesh crinkle with the sound of wrapping paper. One eye rolls back in his head. "Do you, Jack Jupiter, promise to take Darlene Christie as your lawfully wedded wife, to have and to hold until someone bashes out your brains, for worse or for worser, in sickness and in squelch, to love and to cherish, from this day forward until life do you part?"

I don't answer. I am screaming in my head, screaming until I feel nauseous. Suddenly, I feel everyone's eyes on me. I look down at my feet, see a rotten toe sticking out from a hole in the leather. Worms wiggle from it. Maggots shift beneath my loose toenails.

I look at Darlene.

"I do," I say, if only to stop this madness.

"You may now kiss the bride," the priest says.

My hands begin to work on their own. They reach out to grab the veil, and lift.

Now, the screams escape my lungs. Darlene's face is gone. What remains is a shiny, pulpy, bloody mess. Her skeleton shows through. Her teeth are mostly gone. Those that remain are broken and cracked.

Darlene Darlene *Darl*—

"Darlene!" My scream wakes me up. The inside of the trailer is hot and I am soaked through with sweat, but somehow I am shaking, chilled to the bone.

My vision is blurry, still coming out of my sleep. I don't know how long I slept for, but I know I never want to sleep again.

The zombies rustle and groan around me. They are no longer quiet as they were before, but they are also not as loud. In fact, it is not very loud at all inside of the trailer. I realize we have stopped moving. The idling sound of the running engine is off. I hear footsteps, boots thudding concrete, outside of the thin metal walls.

Then I hear Tony's voice as he yelps and the door rattles on its hinges. "Watch it, asshole," he says.

My vision has cleared enough for me to see him almost tumbling into an abyss of great, white light. Then I am blinded.

It is not Butch Hazard who comes into focus. It is just one of Butch's soldiers. He is a middle-aged man who wears splatters of blood on his face like it's a new fashion.

"Both of them?" he asks someone I can't see.

"Yep," a gruff voice answers back. "Spike's orders. Get the young one, I'll take this old fart to him."

The soldier seems to quiver at Spike's name, then he says, "All right," and makes his way into the trailer.

"What's going on?" I ask.

The soldier digs something out of his waistband. It resembles a gun, but I know it's not. It's too technological looking for that. As he gets closer, I see the syringe on the end. That's when I start bucking and kicking out to him. But I am no match with my hands cuffed behind my back and with the zombies all around us, who've now started to match my intensity with their shrieks and groans.

The syringe plunges into my neck. My head cricks and I feel a great burst of coldness dancing through my entire body. He moves out of my way. I see Tony doing much the same thing as I am.

He screams, "Don't let them stick you, Jack! Don't let — "

But it is too late.

The brightness doesn't fade as much as it cuts out. And I am back in slumberland, but this time I don't dream of a zombie wedding.

33

THE CELL I WAKE UP IN IS ABOUT SIX FEET BY SIX FEET. There's straw coming out of the mattress, which is an inch thick set on a concrete slab that takes up most of the right side of the room. There are bars in front of me, like a robot's smile, too close to even attempt to squeeze out of. I hear nothing and almost see nothing.

It is early morning, I think, judging by the sun's faint rays streaming in through a small window at the top of the back wall. I am dazed, hungover, in pain... you name it, and if it's bad, then I probably feel like that.

There is no sign of my group. I start shaking. God, where are they? How many prison blocks would a place like Eden have? I think of shouting out for Darlene, but decide it's not the best thing.

I smell shit and blood and sickness.

In the corner of the cell on the left side is a bucket overflowing with mucky brown water. My own private bathroom — just what I've always wanted.

I stand up on shaky legs, climb up to the bed, and look out the window.

What I see takes my breath away.

Mainly because it is not what I have expected.

A rusty roller coaster sticks up high into the sky, a cart on the track stuck at the top of the hill. There's a larger structure beyond, written down it reads, TOWER OF POWER. I see a circular stadium, rolling mounds of dirt inside of it. I see a Ferris wheel, the green and red paint splotchy and peeling. I am on the fourth or fifth floor of some building, looking out onto an abandoned theme park. There are walls constructed around the edge of land, made of wood and metal, patched and unprofessional, but some of these walls almost reach the midpoint of the Ferris wheel's height. I wonder if they are really there to keep the zombies out and not to keep the people in. Near the back of the fence are houses, the type of houses the government would construct in a low-income area. I've seen many of them in Chicago. They were once nice here, but now they are falling apart. Shattered windows. Shutters hanging crooked. Doors covered by plywood.

Sad.

Closer, I see shuttered buildings with signs like:

GAMES, FOOD, & FUN! ENJOY AN ICE-COLD COCA-COLA! I see some people milling about. They don't look like your typical amusement park goers. There are no smiling faces. Everyone walks like the weight of the world is on their shoulders.

It might have once been a place of fun, but now it is a place of oppression.

"Welcome to Hell's theme park," a voice says, I faintly recognize.

"Tony?" I say. "Tony, is that you?"

"Yours truly," Tony answers. "Heard you shuffling around like a drunk in the dark."

He must be in the cell next to me. I don't see him, but I hear him loud and clear.

"Where is the rest of the group?"

Tony makes a nasally noise like he's weighing the question. "Could be they're dead."

No. No, they're not. Somehow, I know they're not. I'm shaking my head as Tony starts talking again.

"But I doubt it," he continues. "Spike is like a big, dumb cat. He'll play with his food before he eats it. Like *Tom and Jerry*, remember that cartoon, Jack?"

"I do," I say, trying to ignore how crazy Tony sounds.

There's a moment of silence, heavy silence, the kind that feels like it's suffocating you.

I break it with another question. "Who is Spike, Tony, really?"

Tony chuckles. "Best I don't say here. He's always listening." He pauses, the silence deafening. "Eh, fuck it. Spike is a petulant asshole. Rumor has it that he worked here before this shit went down."

I picture a large, muscular man working security or helping build roller coasters.

"Worked in the Old West part of the park as a Black Hat impersonator, you know, the bank robber, the merciless killer."

That image in my head shatters.

"Funny, isn't it? I heard he got so tired of losing in the staged gunfights, he threw a tantrum and shot his cap gun off at the good cowboy, then turned on the crowd and shot the caps off at the families watching. A couple kids burst out in tears and suffice to say, some mommies and daddies weren't very happy 'bout that. He gets the pink slip and it's bye, bye, bad guy."

"So how'd he take over if he's just a punk playing dress up?" I ask. I am leaning up against the wall, a little too close to the slop bucket.

"Because he's crazy and when someone is crazier than a world where the dead are walking around, that person always wins...but I've said enough, I think. You'll meet him soon — "

A door opens at the end of the long, dark corridor. My heart hammers in my chest. Am I going to meet him now? I hate myself for not being ready, for being caught off guard. I will fight if I have to, fight until I am reunited with Darlene and my group.

It is not Spike, but Butch Hazard carrying an AR15 instead. He's smiling, thin skin stretched over his skull, making him look like Death.

He opens the door. Metal grinds as the gears click open

I stand my ground. No longer cuffed. I can fight back.

He raises his rifle. I don't even get to speak before the butt of the gun cracks me against the side of the head. I hit the floor hard, loose straw sticking to my face.

The darkness comes again.

34

I REGAIN CONSCIOUSNESS AN ETERNITY LATER. DIM lights come on with a dull click that echoes in whatever room I'm in. It echoes harder in my head. With this sound, my eyes open. My head is swimming. I feel both tired and rested. Mostly I feel hungover.

It doesn't take long for my eyes to adjust because of what I see in front of me.

It is Darlene and I am relieved she is not a zombie. I lunge forward. "Darlene!" I shout, trying to jump the table and hug and kiss her. No luck. Metal bites into my wrists. I'm handcuffed to the chair, not going anywhere. Go figure.

Darlene doesn't wear a wedding dress and a veil like in my nightmare, but a tank top, the kind with spaghetti-string straps. It is normally a light blue, but has been blackened by blood and sweat and dirt. She is asleep and she always looks even more angelic when she's sleeping.

Between us is a long table made of shiny metal. There are scratches on the surface from what looks like forks and knives. Or maybe this was actually a chopping block.

The fear starts creeping back into my brain, drowning out the relief of seeing Darlene. I try to shake it away but can't.

The door opens, letting in a flood of more light. I catch glimpses of the walls — brick, stained with red, cracked and falling apart.

A shadowy figure is in the doorway. It is either a very large person or two people.

When the figures cross through I see that it is two people. One of Butch's soldiers and Abby. She is awake, stumbling and groggy-looking, but awake. Blood has since dried on her upper lip and from the corners of her mouth.

"Abby," I say. Now the fear goes, replaced by fury. I grip the arms of the chair hard.

She looks at me with a blackened and swollen eye and manages a smile. The soldier guides her into the seat next to Darlene. He pulls the chair out for her and it makes a terrible screeching noise that is enough to rouse Darlene out of her daze.

Darlene takes in a deep breath and her eyes flutter. "Jack?" she says. "Jack, where are we?"

"I don't know," I answer. I feel like I might cry. There's a cloud of happiness swelling inside of me, but inside that cloud, there are streaks of black fear and sadness, threatening to burst.

"My head hurts," she says. "Did we drink another box of wine? I thought we were gonna quit doing that."

I laugh, the sound bursting from my lips. It hurts. Darlene and I used to go to Walmart and buy a couple boxes of Franzia, then at home, we'd put on a B-movie horror flick, get drunk off our asses, laugh at the terrible acting, and fall asleep in each other's arms. Of course...we'd wake up with terrible hangovers and even worse breath, but hey, those nights were fun.

"No, honey," I say.

Darlene's muscles twitch as she tries to bring her hand up to rub her head. She is stopped short by the cuffs.

The soldier offers us a lopsided grin, as if to say, *"Ha-ha, you ain't going nowhere."*

We'll see about that.

More people shuffle in through the open door where the blinding, outside light has dulled to something resembling normalcy. It is Tony being pushed by another of Butch's soldiers. He is thrown into the chair next to me. The cuffs click a million times before the soldier stops pressing down on them. Fresh blood spills from his nose. Through all of this, Tony doesn't show that he is in pain or that he is even out of control. I can't help but admire the man and feel bad for him at the same time.

"Stop, you're hurting him," Abby croaks. Her head lolls back and forth. The soldier pays no notice to her pleas.

"What's going on, Jack?" Darlene asks.

"I don't know," I say, in a whisper. I truly don't and it makes me feel like I'm walking a tightrope between the tops of two skyscrapers, no harness.

"Someone please tell us what's going on!" Darlene squeals.

No answer.

The soldiers make for the door. It starts to shut behind them, the little bit of daylight getting slimmer and slimmer.

We are left without an answer. All four of us are handcuffed to our chairs. There are no windows, only brick walls stained with what I imagine to be blood. And our one escape is closing slowly.

Just as I am thinking this, the door swings open.

Hope swells in my chest, but it's quickly dashed when I see who strolls in through the door. All barrel-chested, standing too straight. Butch Hazard.

"Welcome to Eden," he says. "Bring in the other one."

One of the soldiers appears in the doorway.

I try to jump from my chair, but I'm not going anywhere. Instead, the cuffs cut into my wrists, making a rippling burst of pain shoot up my arms all the way to where the bullet graze wound pulses.

"Norm!" I shout.

It's like he doesn't even hear me. His chin touches his chest, head moving back and forth like a bobblehead. Butch grabs a handful of his hair and pulls him up so he is facing me. What I see almost burns me from the inside out. Norm looks nothing like he did when I last saw him. His face is a pulverized piece of meat. A chunk of his bottom lip is missing. His cheeks are swollen, eyes puffy. He looks like a man with a bee allergy who's fallen in a human-sized nest and has been stung over and over again. I can't help but think this is my fault. Somehow, someway. My fault. I want to scream. I want to cry. And I can't do either of these things. I have to remain composed. Calm. Collected.

"Norm," I say.

"My God," Darlene says. "You're a monster."

Butch chuckles. "No, sweetie. The monsters are outside of these walls. Look on the bright side. If you can stomach a couple punches to the face," he lifts up Norm's hand, which is wrapped with a grimy and blood-soaked bandage, "and a few missing fingers, then you'll be safe from the real monsters."

This is when I realize Norm is missing the index finger on his right hand — his trigger finger. It is cut off to the middle knuckle, causing it to be even shorter than his pinky. The graffiti I saw in Sharon flashes inside my mind: HIDE YOUR FINGERS. I feel like vomiting.

He unhooks cuffs from the back of his pants, and puts them on Norm in the chair next to Abby.

“Hang tight, guys,” he says, “Won’t be long. Spike likes to make these grand entrances sometimes.” He rolls his eyes and shrugs. “What can I do about it? He’s the boss. I just follow orders.”

With that, he leaves.

“Norm,” I say. “Norm!” There’s a happiness in my voice even I can hear despite our current circumstances. He is not dead. He is fucked up, beaten and broken, but he is not dead. And if he is going to die, then at least we can die together.

When the door shuts — and it actually shuts this time — Darlene breaks out in a loud sob.

“Don’t cry,” I say. “It’s all gonna be okay.” But I’m lying. I’ve done more lying to her in the past six months than I have in the prior five years before that. It’s something I have to do. I have to give her hope even when all hope is dead.

She looks up at me, then turns her head to Abby and Norm. “Look at them. It’s already not okay. I thought I could handle this. I thought I could be tough and take whatever they threw at me, but I can’t, Jack. I’m not like you.”

I want nothing more than to get out of this chair and hold her.

"Darlene," I say, trying to muster up a smile. It's not easy. There is no light at the end of the tunnel here. I know that now. I know we will probably die in the very place we were dying to get to.

There is a long, drawn out moment of quiet where all we can hear is Norm's raspy breathing, and the muffled sounds of wheels going over gravel.

"I don't get it," I say. All the beaten faces and hurt eyes turn to me. "Spike got what he wanted. He got Herb. Why does he want us?"

Tony chortles. "It was never really about Herb. Don't get me wrong, the kid is special, but so is a hundred other Edenites. It's about *control*. Spike and Butch crave it, so when a citizen goes missing, they find them."

This causes Norm to stir, his eyes fluttering. The left one holds open, though it is almost swollen shut.

"Spike is not a man who forgives and forgets," Tony continues, glancing at my older brother. Then his voice drops into a clichéd southern drawl. *"He's the rootinest, tootinest, yee-haw, honky-tonk this side of the Mississippi!"*

Abby sits up a bit straighter.

Darlene shakes her head. "He's gone crazy. Look at him."

"No," I say, "he started to say the same stuff back in the trailer."

"Yeah, he was already slipping," Darlene says.

"You'll see," Tony says.

"*Uhhhh,*" Norm says. "Little brother." He tries to smile, his bloody lips peeling back to show red teeth. Some of them are missing.

It hurts me, too, but I smile back at him. "Good to see you again, Norm."

"Listen to Tony. H-He knows what he's t-talking about," Norm says. He smiles again before he closes his eyes and continues his raspy breathing. It's terrible to look at him like this. My brother who has helped protect us for the last six months reduced to a shell of himself.

"Damn right I do," Tony says. "I was here after Spike took over. Norm has seen it single-handedly." Tony laughs. "You'll see. Think Butch Hazard is bad, wait to you get a load of this psycho son of a bitch."

Wait until that psycho son of a bitch gets a load of *me*.

I look at Darlene. Her teeth are chattering. Seeing this douses my anger. Now, I just feel bad for her, for my brother, for all of us.

Abby shakes her head back and forth. "Well, it was nice knowing you guys," she says. "I'm gonna try to die on my own before some psychopath can murder me. So excuse me." She leans her head back as if she's going to sleep.

I got to find a way out of here. I can't let my family die. Not even Tony or Herb.

The door opens and a figure stands beneath the frame, backlit by the daylight. Somehow, he seems to darken this light. This figure wears a cowboy hat.

His voice is an almost perfect echo of Tony's southern imitation. "Welcome, guys and gals, to Eden's first ever reverse dinner party!"

Then he is gone, yelling, "Yee-haw!" as he pushes in a party of zombies.

35

I COUNT FIVE OF THEM. THEY ARE NOT THE NORMAL TYPE of zombies you see strolling around abandoned streets and sidewalks. These are creatures that have almost been domesticated. They wear clothes that are unmarked, unsoiled, and clean. Pristine white jumpsuits. There is little black ink leaking from the corners of their mouths. I notice, in the glare of the light overhead, one zombie woman seems to have a black smear on her chin, as if someone was close enough to wipe the mess away. Their eyes blaze with dark gold, eyes of zombies well-fed. Dare I say, happy zombies?

I jerk in my chair, the chain rattling. This is mostly a reaction rather than an attempt to escape. I know I am not strong enough to break these chains, but the fear and adrenaline coursing through my veins tells me I am.

Darlene's fear and adrenaline must be telling her the same thing because she's about to pop her arms out of her socket to break free.

The zombies inch closer.

Even Tony feels the heat of death licking against his skin. He squirms and shimmies, trying not to get his face anywhere near the approaching dead.

All the while, some man laughs like a cartoonish villain in the background.

Ha-ha-ha-ha-ha!

Think of the Wicked Witch of the West on acid except replace the high, shrill laughs with deep, gruff laughs instead. And except for flying monkeys, we got some lab experiments gone wrong.

I'd take flying monkeys over these bastards any day.

The lead zombie puts his arms out — the *Frankenstein* position — and heads for Norm. He is almost too gone to notice, but not gone enough to die without pain. I hold my breath as this unfolds in front of my eyes. I wait for the rip of flesh, the scream, the sound of blood raining down on the concrete floor, the death gurgling, and the munching. As I wait, I turn my head away and look at Darlene.

She has since given up her mad struggle to break free of the chains.

I say, with my lips quivering, "Close your eyes, Darlene. Picture our life back in Chicago. The pancakes in the morning, the boxes of wine and bad movies. Picture all of the good times." I have to stifle a sob. "It will all be over soon."

She nods, a fresh tear spilling down her face, clearing a small pathway through the dirt caked on her cheeks.

I close my eyes, too, waiting for this all to be over.

36

Once the laughing from near the door stops, I hear nothing besides the sounds of our own labored and frightened breathing.

This is when I open my eyes.

I see Darlene in front of me, her eyes still closed, Abby and Norm next to her, their eyes open as much as their swollen faces will allow but not seeing anything. Behind them, the zombies hover. They look across the table, the one behind Darlene — a middle-aged man with a heavy beer gut now full of dead organs — looks at me, while the zombies behind Norm and Abby look at Tony and the empty seat next to them.

What the hell is going on?

These ravenous beasts have fresh meat right in

front of them, yet we aren't getting torn apart yet. What gives?

Then a voice drifts through the air. That southern drawl. "Now, y'all wanna watch this. This here is a *B-yoot*." There's silence again, but the rattles in the back of the zombies' throats begin to rev up. "Now, Butch!" Spike shouts.

A cold hand touches my neck about the same time the other cold hands touch the rest of my group. I see a flash of light beneath the collar of the middle-aged zombie behind Darlene. It blinks once then twice with the movement. Then it begins to bend over her, its mouth hung open, rotten teeth and thin lips bared.

Truly, I am at a loss for words. Hell, I can't even scream.

But Darlene does when those grayish fingers close around her throat.

"Stop it!" I shout.

Useless words.

This is something Spike and Butch Hazard want to hear. They want me to beg and plead for my life. I thought I was better than that. But when you see the love of your life about to be devoured by a zombie, when everyone you care about are in the clutches of a madman, then you don't know what real fear is. Only then would you understand my desperation, my will to survive.

Here comes the laughter again. *Ha-ha-ha-ha!* I

think to myself that is the last thing I am going to hear besides the sounds of my own vital organs being torn out.

Instead, I hear an explosion, not the type of action movie explosions the American culture was so familiar with before all this shit went down.

No, it's a *wet* explosion.

The sounds of ripe watermelons thrown off a ten story building, splattering below.

We are drenched in blood.

37

My ears ring as if a shotgun went off just inches away from my head. Something stings my eyes. There is a dull, meaty taste on my lips. I cannot bring my hands up to wipe away whatever is dripping down the side of my face. My head is swimming, rocking back and forth on the edge of insanity.

I think I know what happened, but I don't want to admit to myself that it has happened. Part of me thinks dying would've been better than going through *this*.

"Yuck!" Abby says.

"Jack. Oh, my God! Jack...*eeeeeeep!*" Darlene yells.

I open my eyes.

I am both happy and thoroughly disgusted to know that my initial thoughts of what happened were right.

The first things I notice, besides the brains and bits of skull fragments stuck to the steel table like steppedin gum, are the headless zombies standing behind Norm, Abby, and Darlene. Red rivers drip down the fronts of their formerly pristine white jumpsuits. The zombie behind Abby still has part of its spine sticking straight up in the air from the meat-stump where its head was.

Tony gives a great shake beside me, like a dog who's just come inside from a great rainstorm. Bits of blood spray me in a fine mist, rotten flesh slaps the floor.

Darlene is pretty much doused in red. All that is untouched is the hollow part of her eye sockets and the dimples on each side of her quivering mouth.

I am breathing hard and fast, though for how long, I don't know.

But we are alive — *I* am alive.

"I love you, Darlene," I say.

She opens her mouth to speak, but the sound of the door stops her.

My eyes drift over there as a figure dressed in a black overcoat and a black cowboy hat walk in, spurs jangling on the heels of his cowboy boots. He has a smile on his face, and a mouthful of rotten teeth, toothpick hanging from the corner of his mouth. "What an entrance!" he says.

"Here he is. The *rootinest, tootinest* — " Tony begins.

A blur of steel flashes from this man's hands. My heart stops as I focus on the steel. It is an old school six shooter, something a cowboy would've worn on each hip almost two hundred years ago.

"Shut up, Richards. I don't want to have to do ya like Butch did your boy."

Tony shuts up.

"Now," the cowboy smiles, "let me introduce myself." He stands at the head of the table, flicks a way something off of the edge that might be a piece of a forehead or a mutilated eyeball, I'm not sure. "I'm Spike, y'all probably heard about me. I run this here place, been running it for...hmm," he brings the barrel of the gun up to his hairline and scratches. "a while, I guess. People like to call it Eden. I just call it home."

Others would call it Hell, I think.

He finally holsters the weapon. I mean, after all, we're about as dangerous as kittens right now with our hands cuffed and our faces plastered in zombie goo.

"And y'all disrespected my home," he says.

The gun doesn't come out again, but he pulls something free from the back of his pants. On his gun belt is a leather scabbard. If it is any longer, I would think it houses a sword. It doesn't and it isn't. Instead, it's a long hunting knife, the kind Western pioneers used on the great plains to skin buffalo, I'm sure. Honestly, I have no idea, but this Spike guy is a walking, talking cliche. I hear Tony's voice echoing in my head: *Rootinest, tootinest...*

"Which one of you assholes is the leader?"

"I am," I say. I may be cuffed to a chair and covered in rotten zombie brains, but I am no coward. I am Johnny Deadslayer. "Name's Jack Jupiter, pard." I smile and it feels so weird to smile at this point.

"Well, Jack Jupiter, I got some bad medicine for you," Spike says. There is a silence as his flint-colored eyes meet mine. He has a look about him that is crazy enough to make me want to turn away.

I don't.

Norm snorts. It's a painful, fluid snort, but it's also unmistakably his agonized form of laughter. "Bad medicine," he says. "Talk n-normal, jackass."

Spike turns his attention on Norm. "I already took a finger," he says, brandishing that big knife, "now don't make me take your tongue, too."

"Leave him out of this," I say. "I'm the leader of the group, talk to me."

Spike arches an eyebrow, tips his cowboy hat. "Fair enough, friend."

"Good. You got what you want, right? You got Herb, now let us go."

A smile slowly spreads across Spike's face. "Yeah, I got the big blacky, but that ain't what this is about." He barks a short burst of laughter and gets up from the table. I hear his boots squelching in the blood and zombie brains. "No, Jack Jupiter, this isn't about what I want and don't want. See, I always get what I want. That's the great thing 'bout this fucked up world we live in now. Ain't hard to take from the weak," he taps the butt of his pistol, "when you got the steel to do the takin for ya."

He rounds the table, and stands directly behind Norm, then he begins to sidle in between him and Abby. He tips his hat at her and says, "Pardon me, miss." It's such an alien gesture to see this among the brick walls and sterile lighting and statue like zombies. I can't help but think he took a wrong turn in a time machine and ended up here instead of 1850's Texas.

"Jack, the reason you and yours is tied up in some abandoned stock room in my kingdom of Eden is because you disrespected me."

And what does he call this? Chaining, beating, and scaring people who should be guests.

"We just met you!" Darlene squeals. Her face is paper-white, and she is shaking.

"May be, ma'am, but you've been quite acquainted with my right-hand man Butch, have ya not?"

Darlene doesn't answer.

"I wouldn't be proud to call that son of a bitch my right-hand man," Abby wheezes. "He's a murderer."

Spike chuckles. "You gotta be sometimes. I'm sure you ain't squeaky clean yourself, princess."

"Look at them," I say. "Look at the women. They've been beaten. What kind of man administers beatings on women?"

Actual concern shows on Spike's face. "Butch said

y'all were already like that when he found ya. World's tough and all."

"You wouldn't know how tough it is out there when you're hiding behind these walls," I say. "You're about as tough as Butch is worthy of being a right-hand man."

Spike pulls his upper lip in a snarl. "Don't try to act like you know me, boy. You don't."

"Oh, I know a lot about you. I have heard some great things. *Funny* things."

Spike's eyes open wide, a fire igniting inside of them.

"It's kind of hard to be afraid of a guy who runs around playing Cowboys and Indians, dressing up like a poor man's John Wayne. Yeah, Spike, I know you used to work in the Wild West wing of the theme park. I know you got fired because you didn't like losing all the time, that you went off script and shot your cap gun at the White Hat, and when he didn't fall over, you threw a temper tantrum. What was it they compared it to, a kid who didn't get that action figure he wanted for Christmas? Yeah, I think that was it. Then you tried to fight the White Hat and got your ass handed to you on a silver platter. Boy, that was a helluva story, helped the time fly by in your little prison. You're a laughing stock around here. Not even Butch respects you."

I'm smiling now despite none of this actually humoring me. I know I am on thin ice. I do not have the upper hand here. We are this crazy asshole's captives, and he has a gun and a knife, and exploding zombies. So no, this is probably not smart, but what choice do I have?

"Shut your mouth," Spike says. "You shut your fuckin mouth right now." The Southern drawl is gone, replaced by the last semblances of something New York or perhaps New England. It's distorted enough for me to not rightly know.

I feel everyone's eyes on me. Even Abby and Norm, whose eyes are almost swollen shut, have opened theirs as wide as they can. Tony, too — the guy who respects this cowboy the least — is now hardly breathing when I look at him, his face telling me I should've shut up while I still can.

But, of course, I'm not going to shut up. I'm pissed. I'm scared. I'm tired of assholes trying to push me and mine around.

"You are just a figurehead. Butch is the one who really runs this place. He goes out there and does what needs to be done for Eden while you sit back with your feet up, shooting off cap guns."

"Enough!" Spike yells.

The gun comes out in a blur and he wraps his arm around Norm's neck with the hand that holds the hunting blade. "You wanna find out if this here's a cap gun, partner? Want me to prove it to you? This your brother, right? Wanna see what his brains look like?"

I bite down hard enough for my molars to pop and turn to dust. I went too far. My stomach clenches as I think I just put the nail in my brother's coffin.

"No," I say. "I told you to leave him out of this. This is between me and you. Leader versus leader."

Norm's face is screwed up in pain, but somehow I notice him smiling. This son of a gun is beaten, missing a finger, on the cusp of death, and he's smiling. It causes me to smirk too.

"This ain't funny," Spike says. "You disrespect me and I kill. Simple, pard."

I see the murder in his eyes.

I scramble for something to say. I'm no longer fueled by that wave of adrenaline that comes over me in times of great stress and uncertainty. I have to think like Johnny Deadslayer. What would he do? He wouldn't let his brother die. He wouldn't let his group be disrespected and humiliated.

I think back to all the old Western movies Norm and me used to watch before he got too old to hang out with his little brother. *The Good, The Bad, and The Ugly, Tombstone, Once Upon a Time in the West,* these all flood back into my mind. Clint Eastwood snarling across the way at Lee Van Cleef and Eli Wallach, that haunting music playing in the background. Val Kilmer saying, "I'm your Huckleberry," in *Tombstone.* Man, that was the pinnacle of my childhood.

There's one thing I picked up from those movies that I think is useful to me right now.

Spike cocks the hammer back on his pistol. The full *click* stops the words in my throat. Norm is trying to move his head away from the barrel, but he doesn't get too far, being confined and cuffed to a chair and all.

"I'm gonna kill each one of 'em," Spike says. "Make you watch as the walls are painted with their blood. How ya like that, pard? With the girls, I'm gonna go real slow, make it painful, so that even when it's your turn, you hear them screaming in the afterlife." Spit sprays from his mouth as he talks. The toothpick falls and is lost in a pool of dark blood on the table.

"This isn't about them, it's about me. I disrespected you, they didn't."

Norm chuckles then says, "Me, too..." in a weak voice.

That one thing I learned from those Westerns is that a gunslinger won't refuse a gunfight.

Never. Not if you're a *true* gunslinger.

"Now I'm gonna make you pay, pard-na!" Spike bellows. He raises the blade in one hand and grabs Norm's face with the other. The knife presses up against Norm's ear, and he's screaming. It's the sound of a dying man, and it ices my blood. A trickle of red falls down Norm's neck. His features bunch up in pain.

"I challenge you!" I shout. My last hope. "I challenge you to a gunfight. Like the Wild West."

Spike lets the blade drop from Norm's face. He turns slowly to look me square in the eyes.

"You fancy yourself a cowboy, right?" I ask. "Then prove it. Prove to me you're not just playing dress-up because it's the end of the world."

Spike narrows his eyes. His pupils are like steel. "I ain't gotta prove to you a damn thang."

There's a moment of silence lingering between us as we stare, face to face. I know he must have cameras in here. I know Butch Hazard and his crew of soldiers are just beyond the doorway waiting to bust the door down at the first bad sign of things not going in Spike's favor. I know this and so does Spike.

"Not to me, then," I say. "Prove it to your right-hand man and your legion of soldiers. Prove it to the people of Eden. Make them respect you instead of fear you."

"Fear is respect," he says, his tone taking on that of someone who is not getting their way.

"Well, I guess you're not only crazy, but you're dumb, too."

He shoots up from his leaning posture.

Darlene stares at me, not even breathing. I look at Norm and he's exhaling a great sigh of relief as he tries to rub the side of his head on his shoulder, unsuccessfully. Then Spike is up and walking back around the table, blade in hand. The spurs jingle. I am reminded of a dog with a bell on its collar, and I can't help but smile.

"Think that's funny?" he says.

Next thing I know, his leg comes up and he boots Tony's chair — with him still in it. And Tony topples over, not even able to flail his arms for balance. The metal bangs against concrete with a sharp crack, and Tony moans out in pain.

But that is the least of my worries.

Spike grips the arm of my chair, spins me halfway around to meet him. The legs scrape the floor like nails on a chalkboard. Darlene screeches.

"No! Leave him alone!" she yells.

I can't even turn my head and give her a reassuring look, or tell her everything is going to be okay like I have been telling her our entire relationship. Maybe that's a good thing. Maybe she'll finally open her eyes and realize everything *isn't* okay.

"Oh, I'm gonna leave him alone. He'll need to be left alone," Spike says. The normal voice is creeping out again, almost whiny.

He has that big knife in hand and he swings down on my head. I feel a crack, a sickening crack, and warm blood runs down my face.

He swings again.

"Stop it! Stop it! You're hurting him!" Darlene says.

Crack.

"Darlene," Abby echoes. She turns toward my fiancé with a look that says, *stop it before he hurts you too.*

Spike is laughing maniacally. He smiles wide. His teeth are much more rotten this close up. So are the wrinkles in his skin. Probably from hours in the sun, probably from age. I don't know for sure. I just know he's not the most handsome fellow.

He hits me over and over again.

I pass out to the sounds of Darlene's shrieks and Spike's mad cackles.

38

I AWAKE TO QUIET.

I haven't gotten too much quiet these days. Was it all a dream? The room is almost pitch-black, somehow darker than it was when my eyes were closed and I was lost in the deep, dark pools of sleep. The rough straw mattress and hard concrete bed remind where I'm at, but the smell of the slop bucket solidifies it.

My head feels like it's on fire.

I rub at it, feeling the dried blood and the knot. The feeling doesn't go away.

I make a move to get up. My entire body is sore, and not the good kind of sore you get after a tough workout, the kind where you can barely sit on the toilet without thinking, *Fuck, I'm never running again* and *Good job, Jack!* No, this hurt is the kind of hurt I'd expect someone who somehow survived getting hit by a Mack truck to feel. Pain filling every nook and cranny, man.

"Kill me," I try to say, but it comes out in a hoarse whisper. Now I'm realizing how badly I want water. I wonder how long I've been out. The bars on the little sliver of window offer no daylight or moonlight, just black sky and damaged hopes.

"Tony," I say, knowing his cell was close to mine before. Then I speak again, this time the word coming out cleaner. "Tony!"

No answer.

I go back to sleep. I dream of Darlene and Norm. Their dead bodies on fire beneath the forgotten and rusty roller coaster.

I wake, hearing a thud.

Sunlight streams in through the small window, flitting back and forth. Shadow. Sunlight. *Thud. Thud.* Shadow. *Thud.*

I rub at my eyes.

Thud. Thud. Thud.

It continues like an alarm clock. My body is still sore, but my mind is even worse off. I can't help but think of Darlene and Abby and Norm and Tony, even

Herb. If I could just lay here for the rest of my life — which I don't think will be much longer — I'd probably be better off.

But I can't.

Johnny Deadslayer wouldn't. He'd find a way out.

Something wet falls from above me, causing me to stop mid-thought.

Thud. Thud.

Whatever hit me is warm and is dripping down my face. I raise my hand and swipe at it. I look at my fingers. Whatever it is is sticky and red. My heart skips a beat for a moment as I think to myself that it's blood.

But it can't be blood.

Thud. Thud.

A fainter *thud.*

The sunlight drifts in and out of the small cell that has been my home for too long.

Thud.

I turn my head to look at the window.

Now my heartbeat has stopped because what I see on the outside, dangling by a frayed rope, is enough to ice me over completely.

It is Tony.

His face is frozen in a snarl. The only smile I see on him comes across his neck, and it's a deep smile, a red smile. A slit throat.

Thud-thud-thud.

Blood sprays with each hit.

I am standing on the bed now, and my knees go weak, threatening to give out and have me tumble all the way to the piss-soaked, hard floor.

There is also a bullet hole in Tony's head. It is dark and almost perfectly circular. Part of my mind tells me the hole is still smoking as if he has just been executed, but I know that is only my brain playing tricks on me. A thin stream of blood runs from this hole, zigging and zagging down the bridge of his nose then his mouth then finally falling off of his chin in thick, red drops.

"Tony," I say in a whisper.

Around his neck is a sign which looks to be written in his own blood. I TELL LIES AND NOW I'M DEAD.

This is my fault. I never should've opened my mouth about Spike's past. Oh, God. It hurts. A choked sob escapes my throat. If he would do that to Tony, what would he do to my Darlene or my brother or Abby?

I shake my head. No, I can't think like that. I have to be strong. I have to be Johnny Deadslayer.

Rest in Peace, Tony.

The gates rattle down the corridor. A line of light shoots down the hallway as hinges creak. Boots thud against the concrete, keys jingle, and I almost mistake them for Spike's spurs, but I know better than that. He wouldn't subject himself to the cells.

Sunlight catches Butch's face. "Up, Jupiter," he says.

In one hand he has a nightstick, and in the other he has his Desert Eagle.

"Where's Darlene?" I say.

"Don't worry about her, she's safe."

I stand up, knowing the drill. If I even breathe wrong, I'm taking a nightstick into the gut or the butt of the Eagle to the temple.

"I see you got the present Spike left you," Butch says. "It was messy, let me tell you." He leans forward, brings the hand with his gun in it up and whispers, "I told you he was crazy."

"When's my shootout?" I ask. "When do I get to put a bullet in his head?"

Butch stares at me, incredulous. Then he speaks the way a man speaks to a cute puppy, that soothing, comforting tone. "Oh, Jack, you can't be serious. Did you really think he was going to give you an honest chance to kill him?"

"Y-Yeah," I say.

Butch smiles, lifts his eyebrows up. Sweat drops from his buzzed hair and falls down the sides of his face. "Nope, buddy. Sorry," he says and chuckles, his face going serious. "Now turn around. And if you mess up one time, Jupiter, just one little display of funny business then I'm breaking both of your arms. If you want to have any chance of surviving in the Arena, you don't want your arms broken."

There is a time and place for rebellion, and this is not it.

What the hell is the Arena? I almost ask, but don't.

He cuffs me and he's not fragile at all.

Then, he throws a burlap sack over my head that smells like rotten potatoes, and leads me out of the cell, like a pig to the slaughterhouse.

39

WE RIDE ON A HORSE AND BUGGY, THE STEADY *CLOP-CLOP* of the hooves and the creaking of the wooden carriage confirm that for me.

I hear whispers.

"Is that him?"

"The Zombie Killer?"

"The Carnivore?

"He will put an end to that psycho Spike."

"He's come to free us."

"I think he deserves whatever Spike gives him!"

"Be quiet, you old kook!"

It's the whisper of a thousand people, all combined into one.

"ATTENTION CITIZENS OF EDEN, WE WILL BE GATHERING AT THE ARENA IN ONE HOUR. ATTENDANCE IS MANDATORY. ANYONE

CAUGHT OUT IN THE STREETS WILL BE SWIFTLY DEALT WITH."

It's the loudspeaker, but not Butch's voice behind it. Someone else's. Someone much more robotic.

"ATTENTION CITIZENS..." it continues.

We go on, the hooves clopping and the wheels creaking. We stop ten minutes later. There are no more whispers.

Someone grabs me hard by the arm, making the bullet graze bark out in pain. A hand rips the burlap sack off my face.

I am in a room that might've once been a locker room. There's rows of lockers, most of them are empty and open, but the smell of sweaty socks and gym equipment is full. Butch stands in front of a dusty chalkboard, a soldier on each side of him holding their AR15s.

"All right, Jupiter, this is how it's gonna be," Butch says.

Another soldier is behind me. He sticks a key into the cuffs. I hear a click and all the pressure around my wrists is gone.

Butch reaches in his waistband, brings out an old Western revolver, the kind I'd call a Colt Peacemaker but would probably be totally wrong because all I have to go on is my wealth of old Western movies I'd watched as a kid. Butch spins it on his finger. He throws it at me, the gun twirling in the air, catching gleams of overhead light.

I reach out and grab it, coolly, calmly. Like I've been doing this for years.

Butch and the soldiers take to laughing.

Just for the hell of it, I point the weapon at Butch.

Butch freezes up, the soldiers's laughter stopping as abruptly as it started. I cock the hammer and pull the trigger.

Nothing.

A dull *click*.

I'm smart enough to know he wouldn't give me a loaded gun, but I pop the cylinder out anyway. There are six bullets inside. I aim the pistol again, and pull the trigger.

Nothing.

More laughter.

"It's a dummy," Butch says. "Just like you." He belts out another great burst, and the soldiers follow suit. "When the time is right," he says, wiping the tears from his eyes, "we'll get you hooked up with sound effects and smoke, so you don't die looking like a complete pussy."

"What the hell are you talking about?" I ask.

"It's all a set up," Butch says, "I told you that. Spike may be unstable, but he ain't playing with fire."

My grip on the gun gets tighter. I feel the metal biting into my skin, drowning out the pains on my right arm. "I'm not surprised. Where's Darlene? Where's my brother and Abby and Herb?"

"Don't worry about them. You'll see them soon enough. Well...maybe not Herb. Spike sent him to the dungeon."

"The dungeon?" My stomach roils. What kind of sick...never mind. I know who I'm dealing with now.

One of the soldiers snickers.

"It's where we round up the stray zombies. We set a trap about a quarter mile from the gates. They pool up, it's real — ah, never mind, Jupiter. Makes no difference to you. You're gonna be dead. But don't worry, you'll see your friends soon enough."

"I want to see them now," I demand.

Butch grins. "In Eden, you get no say. It's another country — hell, another world — far as you're concerned."

The hopelessness turns to sadness. I think of Darlene, how we are still not married. My brother with his own missing appendage, and Abby is a girl who never got to live a normal adult life. It's all sad. Too sad..

"In all seriousness, Jupiter, it's out of my hands. I don't like you, I don't like your cunt-bag brother or the feisty bitches you associate yourself with, but I respect you and I respect them. Too often in these wastelands, people just bow down to the guys with big guns and numbers. You, Jack Jupiter, you gave us a little fight, you made it interesting. We still win in the end, but man, I doubt I'll find any other assholes like you."

I don't say anything. In fact, I'm not exactly sure what to say. Thank you for respecting me but still ending my life, maybe? No, I just nod and look down at the prop gun in my hand.

"Then let us go," I say. "Maybe we'll meet again."

"I can't," Butch says.

"Why not?"

"In about thirty minutes, you'll see," he says, that familiar smile on his face. "Until then, I say clear your head. When I was carving up towel-heads in Baghdad, my C.O. would have our platoon meditate. Now that was the most pussy shit I'd ever heard at the time, but you know not to backtalk your Commanding Officer if you want your tour to go peachy, so we all did it, and boy, let me tell you it is one of the greatest things a soldier can do. You don't hear the explosions or the cries of pain, you don't think about your wife and kid back home, missing you. None of that bullshit. You don't think about anything at all. And when you come to, you're only focused on the task at hand. In my case that was blowing out the brains of a few sand niggers, but it doesn't matter if you're doing that or if you're killing zombies, or just trying to survive. Trust me, Jupiter."

The soldiers on his sides have gone stone-faced. No doubt, Butch makes them do the same bullshit.

Meditate...get real. Maybe back in the real world but not now.

"We'll let you be," Butch says, he opens the only closed locker on the top row. In it is a complete cowboy get-up, a few shades too dark to be Woody from *Toy Story*. Fucking great, really. "Put this outfit on, clear your head, but any funny shit, and my men standing guard will do worse than knock your lights out?"

He leaves, and when the door closes, I immediately start looking for an escape.

No luck.

I sit down on the floor, my head throbbing, my heart hurting, and I picture Darlene. It's my own form of meditation. She is the only thing that calms me these days.

And I wait.

40

I SIT THERE FOR WHAT FEELS LIKE FIFTEEN MINUTES. There is one window in this room, and it is a lot like the window in the cell I have spent God knows how many nights in — a small sliver with bars on it.

I am trying to fit into this smelly, way too-starched, plaid shirt as something taps on the glass. My stomach clenches with the memory of Tony swinging by a rope, a bullet in his head, blood leaking down his face. I can't look because I know it will be Darlene or Abby or Norm. I don't know where I'm at. I could be on the basement level and Darlene could still be swinging lifeless with a noose around her neck. That's just the way this world works now. Screw the basic laws of physics. Screw logic. Those things go out the window when people catch a killer virus, die, and come back craving brains and human flesh.

But the tapping grows more persistent.

It's not the meaty thud of a body hitting the outside wall. No, this is the tapping of a finger, someone trying to get my attention.

I go against my stomach's wishes and I look up to the small window. There, beyond the small pane of glass, I see Herb's big, smiling face. My own face breaks into a smile. It's great to see someone familiar... someone that's alive.

"Jack! Jack!" he shouts, his voice much too loud. He is laying in the dirt and grass, I see the blades tickling his face. He is covered in blood and muck.

"Shh!" I say, my finger up to my lips. That smile disappears. Now's not the time for fairy tale reunions.

"Jack! I came back. I told ya I would! I got out of that stupid, smelly dungeon and into the lab! Doc Klein told me to run as far away as I could, but I came to help you, Jacky! Help you!"

"Herb, you have to be quiet they'll hear you."

"But you won't hear me through the glass."

"I do, Herb, I hear you."

"You do?" he says, cocking his head. "That's great! Really! Remember when we met, it was a Thursday —"

"Yes, I remember, Herb, but listen, we don't have much time. I need you to help get me out of here."

Herb's eyes drift from the window to the grass. He

starts plucking the blades and chewing on his bottom lip.

"Herb?" I repeat.

"I can't, Jack. I want to, but I can't. I may not be the smartest fella, but Butch is a mean old man and he's guarding the door to the Arena with the whole army and if I get caught then Spike will know and he'll cut my finger off. Oh, God! I don't want my fingers cut off, Jack! How will I be able to play the guitar like my mammy taught me?" His face screws up, his head starts shaking with dry sobs. "Then I have to help Doc Klein escape. He says he's been listening on the radio and there's a man out there who knows the cure to the z-zombie germ and his talents are wasted here in this crazy theme park. He wants to help the world, Jacky! And I want to help you! I just want to help you!"

A cure? Yeah, right, that'll be the day.

I look him dead in the eyes and say, "Herb! Get a hold of yourself! What is going on? Where are they taking me?"

He looks up at me, a gleam in his eyes. "I-I don't know what to call it. It's...it's like a show."

"Good, Herb. Good. Keep going. Where's Darlene and Abby and Norm?"

He smiles. "They are fine, Jacky. I just got back from seeing them. The doc is looking them over and then they'll be at the show, too."

"He didn't hurt them anymore?" My eyes begin to

water. It's almost too good to be true. "Herb, please tell me that's the truth."

Herb nods his head excessively, if he does it any harder, I swear his eyes are apt to fling from their sockets. "No. No more. Spike said he doesn't care about them. He only cares about you. Doc Klein talked about it in the lunch room while I was working on the bodies. I heard him, I did! He says you royally p-i-s-s-e-d him off. Made him look stupid in front of Butch and the soldiers. Said they don't respect him no more and he feels like their respect is winning — no — *waning* already. Then he told the people that live here that you were one of those mean, old, nasty Carnivores. But I said, 'No, he ain't!' then I heard him talkin 'bout the cure in Washington D.C!"

A smile creeps across my face, and somehow even that small gesture hurts me. I'm just hurting all over the place. "Thank you, Herb. That is really good to hear about my friends," I say. "Now tell me what I'm getting into and how the H-E-double hockey sticks I can't get out of it."

"You're welcome, Jacky," he says with a big grin on his face. "Okay, they make all the citizens sit in the big place with the dirt floor, you know, where the dirt bikes go *vroom vroom* and there's hills and old stands that used to sell hot dogs but don't sell nothing no more." He frowns at that.

I know exactly what he is talking about with Eden

being an abandoned amusement park and all. I remember those days at a local fair or carnival where I'd be walking with Norm and the sound of the dirt bikes ripped through the air and the smell of diesel and exhaust almost choked me. I loved it. They came from the track where all the rednecks would gather around in their Confederate flag shirts, Budweisers in hand. I never got to experience it. Norm wouldn't allow me — or rather he was too busy hanging with his friends and chasing the girls, which is odd to think about now knowing he's gay. I guess it was all for show. Plus, I saw the arena from my cell window. That's good.

"They did it with Alex and Tom. It was bloody, Jack, so bloody I had to cover my eyes like my auntie would make me do at them scary shows when the monster killed the good guys. Spike's the monster, Jacky. He is. Lawd, he is."

"It's okay," I say. "I'll be okay."

But my voice is breaking up. I can't lie to myself. I can lie to everyone else. Not me.

"I know you will, Jack, I just know it!" Herb shakes his head and puts his hands together as if he is about to pray. I'm expecting him to start giving me a spiel about the Lord up in the Kingdom of Heaven, how with God all things are possible, but he doesn't. "I know you'll be because I made sure of it, Jack. I did!"

"Herb, not so loud — "

He snaps his head to the left.

Somewhere deep in the maze of hallways, I hear the clank and rattle of a door opening and closing.

"Oh no oh no oh no," Herb says. He starts to get up. I can't see much, but I catch a glimpse of boots quickly coming into focus. They are brown boots and they are dotted with drops of blood. Herb starts screaming out, "No, I'm sorry I'm sorry — " while he tries to scramble up, but that boot strikes him in the ribs. He is a big guy, but he retreats into the fetal position like a man being attacked by a bear.

"Sneaking out, are we?" It's Butch. "Tsk, tsk, Herbert. Spike will not be pleased. He might even have to take one of your fingers, maybe a toe."

"No! Not my toesies! Please!"

"Herb!" I shout. "What was it? What did you do?"

He looks at me as the boot strikes him again, causing his face to bunch up in pain. I think I hear a crack of steel-toe against bone, maybe even breaking it.

"Stop it, you bastard!" I shout.

Butch starts laughing that laugh that I've grown to hate more than any zombie. He kicks him again and again. But Herb looks up, tears flooding his eyes, blood trickling down his mouth, and he says, "Salvation comes from the heart." And as he is ripped up from the grass, he taps his chest on the left side.

Great, nothing like some religious babble before I die. *Salvation comes from the heart,* what the hell does that even mean?

"Remember Sal, Jacky! Remember Sal — " Then he is screaming again, crying out for his auntie and his mammy, saying, "Please don't take my toesies. Please! Please!" his voice fading.

Then it's Butch, "All right, Jack, time's up. No more of your bullshit."

The door out of this place starts to open up. I think it'll be Butch with his AR15, ready to beat the ever-loving snot out of me, teleporting like some evil wizard, but it's not. It's just another soldier. For a moment, I think I could take him. He is probably younger than me, his face patchy with a wiry beard. I'm guessing twenty, maybe twenty-two, definitely closer to Abby's age. He snarls at me, baring teeth that have definitely been adorned with braces his parents paid for in the old world. It's an empty gesture, and my confidence soars. Yeah, I can definitely take him, then I can get to Darlene and Norm and Abby, save the day. Just like Johnny Deadslayer.

"No need for that funny business," the kid says. He has his gun raised, pointing straight at my heart.

Kid. He can't be much younger than me and I'm calling him 'kid' like I'm an eighty-year-old asshole. Funny what the end of the world does to you.

"I know you're thinking you can take me, and you're probably right, but there ain't no point in doing that. It'll just end bad for the both of us. We know about you, we know you're a smart 'un. So don't prove us wrong."

The fire goes out of me as fast as it came. Still, in the back of my mind, I hear the dull thuds of Butch's boots clobbering Herb as he cries out.

"You're right," I say. "I don't plan on dying in this fucking get-up."

The kid flashes a smile. "Ain't your Sunday's finest, that's for damn sure."

Butch comes in from out of the shadows. "Nice job, soldier!" he says.

"Sir, thank you, sir!" the kid replies.

Butch turns to me. "I know you didn't plan on that little powwow with Herb, but it's gonna cost him a few fingers, maybe even a hand. So I want you to think about that. Now, are you ready to die, Jack Jupiter?"

"Hell no," I say.

"That's too damn bad. You're gonna die whether you're ready or not."

I smirk at Butch and his soldier and say, "Good luck."

41

By the time they put the hood on me, the sun had gone down. They guide me to the horse and cart again, cuff my hands and throw me on a bed of straw. I land funny on my back, smashing my head, which aggravates every ache in my body.

Time goes by in a pain-induced haze.

Now, someone forces me up. "What's with the hood over my head?" I ask. "I know where we're at."

"Intimidation," someone says. I recognize it as the soldier from the locker room, the kid.

Beneath the sack, I roll my eyes.

Then, I feel a gun in my back, and a different soldier tells me, "It's showtime."

I cannot see much beyond dim light coming through the cloth. I smell dirt and mud and my own fear draped all over me like it's cologne. I hear a constant drone of babbling voices, of a crowd settling into their seats before the show starts. When the dim light grows brighter and the heat from them is baking, the crowd picks up their decibel level. Beneath my feet, the ground changes from concrete to dirt.

Someone cheers to my right, and shouts my name, but the cheer is quickly cut off. To my left, someone else cheers. This one is not cut off. More people chime in. The noise begins to sound like the rolling and crash of tidal waves to my ears. It's a small portion of the people, most of them seem too scared to do much of anything, but it helps ease the fear.

The gun's pressure on my back vanishes, then a hand grabs the sack on my head — along with a handful of my hair — and yanks. White floodlights blind me. It takes a long time for my eyes to adjust.

The arena is a large circle of dirt. Stadium seats surround me, rising above the ten foot wall between dirt and seats, three-hundred and sixty degrees. There are people in almost everyone of those seats. My guess is around a thousand of them. I never thought a thousand people would've survived.

I am at one end of the dirt circle, dressed in my cheap cowboy outfit, and at the other end, raised on a platform, sitting in a makeshift throne made out of what looks like bone, is Spike. He gets up, his dark eyes blazing at me from across the way, which can't be much more than two-hundred feet. He is wearing the same outfit he wore when he bashed my head in, except now he looks rested, shiny, and new. On each hip, slung low, are the heavy, old-school revolvers. They shine.

"Jupiter," someone says from behind me.

I find that I am frozen in place. Even in the heyday of my writing career, the biggest event I did was around two-hundred and fifty people, and they were all spread out in a college auditorium, which didn't make it intimidating at all. Now compared to this —

Someone walks up behind me.

The ice thaws, and I turn to see my own gun belt in the hands of a middle-aged soldier. This belt only has one revolver. The leather is cheap and plastic-looking, something you'd get at a costume shop, and the gun is so obviously fake. They didn't even bother to remove the orange cap at the end of the barrel. The soldier starts putting it around my waist, moving my cuffed hands out of the way. I turn and see the empty look in his eye, this is a man who doesn't care what the hell happens today. Maybe I can use that to my advantage. "Good luck," he says, and walks back to the entrance we came through. Him and his partner pull a barred door across the threshold, locking me in here with piles of dirt and a madman.

I turn back, look down at the gun belt. I barely feel it around my waist. It must weigh about two pounds.

"Jupiter! Jupiter! Jupiter!" some of the crowd starts chanting.

With the belt clasped and my fake pistol hanging from my hip, I smile to the crowd and a small section of them start screaming louder. I look for Darlene or Abby or Norm, even Herb, but all I see are faint shapes and outlines with the floodlights distorting their features.

Feedback from a microphone.

I cringe, my heart taking a great leap inside of my chest.

"Quiet! Quiet!" Spike says. He is standing on his throne of bones, his hat tipped back so he can see each and everyone of his people.

The crowd's noise begins to simmer down to a faint drone — faint enough for me to hear my heartbeat hammering.

"Those of you who cheer, why do you do so?" His Southern drawl is gone. He sounds normal, maybe even educated.

"Because you're a dick!" someone shouts, but who it is, we'll never know. A few people answer that voice with cheers. One of the soldiers behind me chuckles.

"Quiet!"

They do this time, completely — perhaps sensing how unstable Spike is. After all, he has two guns, and they have none. If he just starts firing into the crowd...

"Now, y'all gathered here today because we're

gonna bring a traitor to justice." The fake accent is back and worse than ever, amplified by the microphone.

This is answered by a few cheers. Not many. Things aren't looking too terrible for me. He wouldn't kill me in cold blood, not with more than half the crowd on my side.

"Strike that," Spike says, "*Traitors,* plural."

I feel my blood pressure rising. The pain in my head and the wound from the bullet graze starts to throb with my heartbeat.

"Jack Jupiter is no hero. Jack Jupiter is one of the Carnivores and so is his ragtag bunch of assholes." Spike lowers the mic, expecting the crowd's reaction, and boy, does he get one. A domino effect of gasps ripple through the crowd.

"BOOO!" someone shouts. *"Kill him! Kill him!"*

Okay, odds are no longer in my favor. Not a big deal. I can still dig my way out of this...I think.

"Yes, it is true," Spike says, sweeping his hand out to the crowd. The lights are really growing hot now. I'm sweating, shaking, you name it. I really don't want to die looking like Woody from *Toy Story.*

"We all know the Carnivores are ruthless." He takes his hat off, holds it on his chest, says, "Rest in peace to the Chekov family. We all know about that, I don't think I need to remind y'all about how the Carnies ate them for dinner."

The row closest to me is full of people bowing their heads. Some of the others stare at me as if I am the devil.

"Jack Jupiter here took part in the robbery two days ago in Sharon. Y'all know the one I'm talkin 'bout, the one which coincidentally killed Mel Francis and Dan Carnegie. Now we ain't got no medicine, and Sharon is lost. Can't step foot there without gettin shot at by Carnivores." He flips his hat back on his head, grimaces at the crowd. "Now, I don't know 'bout y'all, but I get pretty bored all cooped up in here like chickens in a cage waitin to be slaughtered! I lose sleep thinkin there's bastards like Jack Jupiter and his gang killin our people and takin our medicine and food just because they can! I think it's time we get some revenge."

The crowd erupts.

"Bring him here!" Spike shouts.

One of the soldiers walk up behind me and nudges me forward. I don't hesitate. With the crowd booing and jeering, I am no longer frozen. There's a time and a place to freeze, and this is not it. I walk, Spike's screwed-up face getting closer and closer.

He holds a hand up. The soldier's grip around my arms squeezes me tighter and I stop.

Spike looks away from me with his blank, dark eyes and scans the crowd again. "See, I'm fair. Jack Jupiter has a gun on his hip. So do I. We are going to do it like they did it back in the day. Back in the Old West. Whoever's fastest on the draw walks away the winner. I'm gonna show each one of y'all here tonight that ain't no carny a match for me."

The crowd cheers again. They love this stuff. I can see it in their eyes now that I'm closer. It's funny that when the world goes to shit, the people go with it.

"But first we're gonna have fun with Jack Jupiter." Spike cocks an eyebrow, "I mean, after all, he could win the shootout. Not likely, but possible, right? So we gotta get some of that sweet revenge, don't we?" He looks to one of the dark tunnels in the circle where the microphone's cord disappears to and he motions to someone I can't see. "Bring 'em out! Bring 'em out!"

I look on with wide eyes, knowing exactly who he is talking about.

They are in cages like animals. The cages are on wheels. Each one of them has a burlap sack over their heads like I had, but they are not cuffed. They are too beaten for them to fight back. That much I can see.

"Darlene!" My breathing speeds up. I feel like I'm looking down on this terrible situation, helpless.

"Jack? Jack? Jack!" she screams. "Help me!"

"Many of you have heard about the rumors of what goes on in Dr. Klein's lab. I'm going to tell you the bulk of those rumors are untrue," Spike says, the accent gone. I wonder if he consciously does this or if it's just a sign of his insanity. "One of them is true. We are working to develop the zombies into soldiers for your protection, and so far our efforts have taken great strides in the right direction, but without test subjects to use our experiments on, we will never know. As is common in all experiments, there are failures. But here in Eden we still have use of 'em." A smile splits his harsh face in half. "Tonight we find out if that's true!"

The crowd is quiet. They are as stunned as me.

One of the soldiers shifts uncomfortably to my right. I don't see him, but I feel him.

Butch walks the dirt between the cages. He looks at me.

"Let them out," Spike says.

Butch takes keys off of his belt, and starts jimmying the locks.

"Now before y'all get squeamish," Spike says, "remember these are the same people who massacred our own in Sharon, the same people who may be the reason your mom or dad or husband or wife dies from a fever or a bad cut! Even your kids! Remember, people! Remember!"

With that, he drops the mic and sits down on his chair, which is not actually made of bones — not human bones, at least — but ivory instead.

First, Norm hits the dirt, a dust cloud billowing around him. He struggles to get up to his knees. As he does. Butch rips the burlap sack off of his head. My heart breaks looking at my older brother's face. It is swollen and blue. There are cuts crusted with blood. One eye is shut completely. Still, just like he did back in the interrogation, exploding zombie head room, he smiles with a few missing teeth.

Abby is next. She kicks and bucks, eventually getting out herself. The soldier guiding her grows impatient, his face snarling, and he throws her. She falls, not as hard as Norm but pretty hard.

"Fuck you," she seethes.

The soldier just smiles.

Behind all of this, Spike cackles like a witch.

Last is Darlene, and the rough way Butch takes her arm causes me to lunge forward. The soldiers behind me grab my cuffed wrists. "Uh-uh, Hercules," he says.

"Jack!" Darlene says, but she sounds so distant.

I'm pulled up to my feet.

The crowd is growing restless, the heads and bodies are constantly shifting from foot to foot. They want blood now. The preliminary matters are too boring. They think they are cooped up chickens, when really they are safe behind these walls, they are blessed.

Butch takes the sack off of Darlene's face.

She tries to run over to me. No luck. Butch holds her back.

"Murderers!"

"Kill them all!"

I see Spike leaning in his chair like the class clown.

He is smiling, his hands up, fingers waggling to the crowd, urging them on.

Keep it coming, c'mon, let 'em hear it, his face says.

"Jack, I love you," Darlene says.

"I love you, too," I say. We stare at each other for a long moment, the crowd buzzing all around us.

"How cute," Norm says, snickering.

Butch sucker punches him, a spray of blood escapes his clenched teeth, and he falls to his knees on the dirt.

I lunge again.

"When are we going to kill these sons of bitches?" Abby asks.

Smack.

She is backhanded by a portly man wearing the soldier attire. A stream of blood falls from the corner of her mouth, and she looks at him. "I'm going to remember that," she says. And she will. I know what she's capable of, but seeing someone hit her brings my rage back.

The portly man just laughs.

Spike picks the microphone back up. "You know, I've punished him once already." He looks to the soldier holding me. "Uncuff him and put his hands in the air! Make him bow down to me!"

The soldier uncuffs me, the pressure vanishing sweetly. But he grabs my hands hard and thrusts them up hard enough to make my shoulders pop. I try not to let him do it, but I'm overmatched. Bowing to Spike makes me want to vomit, but I do.

To the soldier, Spike says, "Bring Jupiter below my feet, and don't let him look away."

The soldier nudges me.

"Now bring my babies out!" Spike says.

Butch seems to grow a shade paler. I see the beads of sweat standing out on his forehead in the sickly light blazing above us. He motions to a couple of his posse near the tunnel.

The crowd goes silent.

There is a terrible buzz that fills the air. In the darkness a red light flips on, the color of the devil, the color of blood.

Dirt starts to shift below our feet. In the middle of the arena, it looks as if a great worm is trying to break through to the surface. The ground shakes. Feedback whines from the microphone, but not loud enough to drown out Spike's mad cackles.

My heartbeat is thrumming in my ears. Darlene looks to me. Norm is too dazed. Abby is trying to stay balanced.

A cage raises from an opening in the dirt floor. Gears and pulleys whine and grind. The top of the dome comes first, its polished metal gleaming. Then comes the rest. The bars are thick, the surface area is large, and the amount of zombies inside is shocking.

It stops and settles, clouds of dirt puffing up around its steel beam underside.

For a second, everything is normal.

The crowd doesn't make a sound aside from a few people asking each other what the hell is going on.

Like a warning siren knifing through the air, I hear it, that noise that only used to be in my head but is now inescapable. I am not imagining this. As much as I wish I was, I'm not *not* seeing zombies milling about in a cage that seems to materialize out of nowhere. I'm not *not* hearing the groans and moans of the dead.

42

THE CROWD GOES FUCKING BONKERS. REALLY, IT'S LIKE their favorite baseball player just hit a walk-off grand slam to win the World Series. Have these people never seen a zombie before? No way. The dead are everywhere. Sure, these walls and gates and crazy bastards with AR15s might keep the hordes out but the people had come from somewhere, some overrun city, right? I'm not crazy to think that, am I?

I curl my fingers into fists. The very reaction of this crowd, who I felt bad for at one point being at the beck and call of this crazy, Brooklyn cowboy, pisses me off. They are no different from the beasts on the outside and the beasts in this pit.

"Yee-haw!" Spike shouts. "That what you want? You're damn right it is!"

The crowd roars again.

"Bring Jack closer to me. We are both gonna wanna see this in all its excruciating glory."

I am jolted off my feet and dragged toward the cage. I glance behind me before the soldier snaps my head back, and I catch the flinty eyes of Spike. There's evil in those eyes, malice. It's as if I'm staring into the face of the devil. He grins wide, sits back in his chair and grips the arms while a small group of camouflaged-wearing jackasses begin struggling to move the platform, their faces turning beet-red, sweat gleaming from their foreheads.

Meanwhile, the crowd goes crazy again.

Me, well, I do what any man in my position would do, any man who is getting dragged to a container full of starving zombies, I go slack, let all my weight fall to my knees. I picture a rock breaking the surface of a pond, sinking, sinking, sinking. I picture a dog on a leash at the vet's office pulling in the opposite direction of that glass door with the doctor's name stenciled on it.

Sadly, the soldiers aren't having any of that, and as they kick me and yank me, the crowd only grows louder.

"Bring the others," Spike says from behind me.

Coming from my left is Darlene, Norm, and Abby. They are fighting, but not with much luck. We are vastly outnumbered now, and it's not like before. On the outside, we're always outnumbered. There were seven billion people on this planet when the disease hit, and I remember hearing reports of an almost ninety percent communicability, which means there's a possibility of over six billion dead people walking this earth. You're always outnumbered, man, I just never thought I'd be outnumbered inside these walls.

Darlene offers me one last look of despair as she passes by, and she's so close I can almost smell the sweetness of her skin.

Jack, she says. I don't hear it over the roaring of the crowd, but I do read her lips. *Jack, I love you.*

"Bring 'em closer," Spike yells. Even with the microphone picking up his voice, I can hardly hear him. But I feel the rough hands pushing into my back. My heels dig into the dirt, making small divots. It's no use. I feel the opposing forces giving.

The zombies look up with their rotting faces, their hands clenched on the bars. I see one with a missing index finger, just like Norm. There is another without eyes, and it looks so weird without the glowing orbs in its face — somehow more dead.

"See that?" Spike says. "This is what you get for messing with Eden. This is what *you* all get!" This is no Brooklyn or Old Western accent. This is the accent of a man who's frayed rope of sanity has snapped a long time ago.

"Throw them in, and make Jupiter watch his friends and his lover torn to pieces," Spike says.

The crowd cheers. They all stand up, the bleachers beneath their feet creaking, their eyes widening.

The soldier's grip on my arms is sweaty. It's a hot night in Florida.

Darlene screams out as she is the first dragged to the zombie cage.

"No!" I scream.

"Yes! Yes!" Spike says. I see him jumping up and down out of the corner of my eye like an overexcited puppy. "Kill them! Kill them all!"

We stop at the base of the platform, about ten feet from Norm and Abby, farther from Darlene who is at the cage's retractable door. The crowd is now on tiptoe, shielding their eyes from the blazing floodlights.

Butch leans over and says in my ear, "I take it back. Tony was lucky. He got off easy. No torture, hardly any pain. These ones....eh, not so lucky. The girl's are always the worst. They scream and scream their damn heads off..."

He drones on, but I don't hear him. All I can do is look at Darlene, the woman that I love about to be thrown into a cage full of zombies while a screaming crowd cheers for her death.

No.

That's it. Fuck this.

It is not hard to make a move against Butch because he is not expecting it. He is scary, he has weapons and a killer instinct I cannot begin to comprehend, but he does not have what I have going for me.

He doesn't have stupidity.

Yeah, that's right, I just called myself stupid. And as I rip my arms out of his sweaty grip and he and his soldier's mouths turn into shocked Os of surprise, I can't help but realize how utterly dumb I am.

But it all happens so fast.

A soldier clears a path in the dense forest of dead limbs and snarling faces inside of the cage with what looks like a six-foot animal catch pole. Another has Darlene by the hair and throws her in. What's even stupider, as I shove my way past Butch Hazard and the younger soldier who I met in the locker room, is that I go in after her.

And the crowd goes wild.

43

THE FIRST THING I HEAR AFTER I HEAR DARLENE AND me hitting the metal floor and the sounds of the curious snarls — as if these zombies' prayers were answered and fresh meat materialized from the heavens — is Spike saying, "You idiots! You imbeciles!"

One of his pistols cracks the night air, seemingly splitting the atmosphere in two. The crowd's screams momentarily quiet. The zombies turn their heads toward the sound of the shot, giving me a moment to scramble up from the floor. My head is thrumming and Darlene is a crumpled ball behind me, but we are relatively unscathed.

"Darlene, get up, c'mon!" I say. I'm scrabbling at her like a dog trying to find a bone he buried in the dirt. "Please! Get up!"

She starts to move. Slowly, but she's moving nonetheless.

From my vantage point I can see the citizens looking on with eager eyes. Salivating. Wanting the kill.

Darlene gets up, dazed, her head lolling from side to side. Then, she snaps to attention. I think it's the smell that hits her first, the rotting smell of dead people. It can get your attention real quick.

"Get him out! Get him out! Get him out right now! I don't want him eaten, I want him to watch. *I want him to watch,*" Spike yells, then breaks into his southern drawl. "Time here's a-wasting!"

He is right, it's a-wasting and it's already wasted because the zombies no longer care about the gunshot of the cheering crowd or the screaming Spike. No, all they care about is us.

There's a fat one with a belly that hangs over his waistband. The bottom part of his jaw is missing. What is left is just a great, red wound speckled with shards of teeth. The top teeth are still sharp, still deadly. Next to him, lunging forward on an ankle that is mostly broken, is a woman who is less rotted than the rest. She must have recently turned. She is a brunette. From a distance, you might even mistake her as normal. But when she opens her mouth and you see the inky-black saliva dripping down her fangs, you realize she is anything besides normal. Next to her, is a man in a greasy trucker's cap and equally greasy — maybe greasier — coveralls. On his chest, stitched in cursive is a name. SAL, it reads. On Sal's left is a man long dead, so rotted, I couldn't even give you an estimated age of this guy. His skin is the color of a fish's underbelly. Most of his head is cracked open, revealing pinkish-gray brains, dried, crusted blood. I immediately think of Pat Huber, my high school bully and how his head looked after I drove the wrong side of a hammer into his open head wound. I shudder. There's a man in a ripped and dirty prison jumpsuit. A woman in a dress that might have once been white. A police officer *(I think of Doaks and Beth coming at me in the Woodhaven Rec Center),* an old woman whose skin sags off her face in droopy folds *(I think of my dead mother).*

And there is more, but I don't get a long enough look at them to really see what they were before disease, bite, death, or whatever took them. All I know is their eyes are glowing, they're hungry, and we are trapped.

44

THE CROWD IS IN CONTROL NOW. THAT MUCH IS TRUE. Spike stands up on his throne, his arms out to his sides as if letting their screams and cheers and jeers run over him like rainwater. "You like this?" he shouts into the microphone, causing a ripple of feedback to slice my eardrums. My back is pressed into Darlene and her back is pressed into the bars. I hear her grunting, the breath whooshing out of her as I am backed up farther and father.

"You want more?" Spike screams.

"Stop it! Stop it, you sadistic fuck!" Abby says, barely audible over the crowd. I want to scream with her. Then I want to put a bullet in Spike's head.

The cowboy is beaming.

A strong wind blows in the arena — a welcome one

— taking his hat nearly off his head. It moves the stench of death away from Darlene and me.

"We have to fight," I say. "We can't go out without a fight." I say this to myself more than anything.

The dead are inches away from me. No heat radiates off of them. Not anymore. Not like it was when the disease ravaged their bodies. I remember the baking corpses in Atlanta when the shit really hit the fan. You could crack an egg and fry up some hash browns on those dying people, no joke. These zombies, well, they're about as cold as ice.

"Y-Yeah," Darlene says.

I break free from her, going head first into a sea of dead. My goal is not to survive, but to clear a path large enough for her to escape.

The bottom of my boot meets the prisoner's knee, and the skin and bone is brittle. It cracks like a twig. I'm not *that* strong, even after life on the road for six months, but if you saw the way his knee explodes out of the side of his leg, you'd think I was the fucking Incredible Hulk.

The zombie lets out a choppy shriek. Of pain? Of confusion? Of defeat?

Meanwhile, the crowd is chanting: *"We want blood! We want blood!"* And they're jumping up and down, thudding against the bleachers.

The door to the cage squeals open, but none of the zombies notice. They are too focused on Darlene and me. A soldier, the one with the scraggly, patchy beard is entering. He looks as gray and squeamish as one of the dead. He has the pole in hand, one with the wire loop at the far end.

"Get Jupiter out of there! Get him out!" Spike yells. "But don't hurt my babies!"

I'm going to do more than that. I'm going to kill them all.

"We want blood! We want blood!"

The snarls of the zombies fill my ears.

"Get him! Get him now!"

Another scream, this one outside of the cage. Through the bars, I see Norm spring up off of his knees. It's a jerky movement, one that would've been much smoother had he not been beaten and tortured, but still an effective one. He throws his head back and connects with Butch Hazard's face and Butch staggers backward, blood gushing from his nose. Norm rolls forward, swipes his leg beneath one of the three remaining soldiers, taking him down. Abby sees this all and must be inspired because her elbow suddenly connects with the gut of the female soldier who is guarding her. The soldier doubles over and her gun goes off, sending sprays of dirt up from the ground.

"We want blood! We want blood!"

Well, they're getting it, and they're going to get more.

But cheers? Can you believe that? Happy, smiling

people in the crowd. I should've realized what kind of people were living here once I saw who Spike really was. Not even Tony would recognize the crowd now. He wasn't anything like *this.*

Sal, the dirty mechanic is eyeing me, sizing me up, for some reason oblivious to all the maelstrom going on outside of the cage. I am side-stepping, sizing him up, too.

"Get him!" Spike shouts.

I'm not sure if he is talking about me inside of here or Norm out there. But the soldier answers back. "I'm trying, damn it!" His voice a high-pitched shriek. So loud, I hear it perfectly clear over the buzz of Spike's microphone, the shouts of the crowd, and the revving-engine sounds of the zombies.

The fat zombie notices that today might be his lucky day. Not only did food plunge into the cage once, but twice. It spins around and grunts a small, quizzical grunt. The soldier freezes on the spot, his back against the cage, hands gripped tight on his AR15 that was slung on his shoulder. He has since dropped the pole with the wire loop. Then, he makes a move for the door, but he only gets it about halfway open before the fat zombie falls on him with a wet plop.

He screams, and the screams are loud, ear-piercing. The rest of the zombies take notice, all of them except Sal who only flicks his head in that direction and looks back to Darlene and me.

"It's okay," I say, "we can get past him. Follow my lead."

She squeezes my waist.

Behind Sal, the zombies are piling up on the soldier. His skin rips, blood spurts like a hot, red fountain. There's the wet squelching noise of claw-like hands digging into his guts. The AR15 goes off in intermittent bursts, its bullets hitting the metal bars with a high-pitched whine, sparking in every direction. Still, over all this chaos is the chant: *"We want blood! We want blood!"*

Sal makes his move, and so do I. I fake right, his whole body lurches that direction, and I dart left, my hand wrapped around Darlene's. Then, I slingshot her toward the door. "Go!" I shout. "Get out of here! I'm right behind you."

Norm stands over Butch Hazard. He swings down, his fist connecting with his face. Butch shouts out in pain. I never thought I'd hear this man of steel cry out, but I do. I know my brother is a badass from firsthand experience. He may be missing a finger and damn near on the cusp of death but he's Norman Jupiter.

You don't mess with the Jupiters, not anymore.

Darlene's movement is choppy, she is trying to judge the distance between here and the freedom of the outside. It's a jump not even I could make, and she realizes this at the last moment. So instead of jumping, she steps on the great, squishy back of the fat zombie, pressing him down on top of the screaming soldier, and then she hops off into the dirt arena beyond the steel cage.

With Sal behind me, I make my own move. The fat zombie is momentarily distracted from his meal after Darlene uses him as a stepping stone, but I go anyway, step right on his face, feeling the exposed inside of his broken-jawed mouth squish beneath my feet. As I am in the air, the cheers from the crowd rocking me, spurring me forward, I see the younger soldier is nothing but a mess of blood and bone. The zombies have stripped most of his meat from his body. He has managed to kill a few, but just one is enough to rip him open. The hot smell hits me like an uppercut, but then it's gone, and my boots are slamming down on the dirt floor and into a warped form of freedom. Before I turn and run, I grab the metal door and try to slam it shut. It does, but I don't hear the latch fall into place. It's enough for now, at least. It will slow them down while I kill the rest of these Eden bastards.

Spike is off his chair now. He looks angry, but he also looks bored.

"I have to do everything myself, don't I?" he says.

I make a move for Butch Hazard's assault rifle which has skittered close to the opening of the steel cage. I go with my right hand, feeling a stab of pain in my ribs.

Darlene is to my right, she is trying to pull Abby off

of the female soldier, who is no longer fighting back, but just laying there and taking Abby's barrage of hits.

Stand, I think to myself, *stand and take whatever comes to you like a man.*

But I've come this far.

The AR15's metal is cold in my grip and as I pull myself up — to stand — Spike's gun goes off.

The crowd gasps. It's like we are performers in a play and they are the audience who is supposed to laugh when something is funny, cry when something is sad, and gasp when tensions are high. They're right on cue. Tensions are really fucking high.

The bullet smacks the metal of the gun, blowing it out of my loose grip, sending it dancing twenty feet across the dirt. The vibrations are like bee stings in the palm of my hand.

He shoots again. His movement is a blur, much too quick for the naked eye, and another slug punches the gun away from Abby and Darlene, sending it flying farther than the one I almost had.

I look at Norm and Butch, anticipating where the next shot will go, but when I look, I see the roles have reversed. Butch is now pinning Norm down. Norm is grunting out, his arms up to block his face from the blows that are raining down on him. Butch grabs his gun, which isn't an AR15, but the chrome Desert Eagle.

"Should I kill him?" Butch says.

"No, they're mine. They're all mine," Spike says,

"'cause I gotta do everything myself, don't I?" His accent wavers somewhere between southern and Brooklyn. He is like a malfunctioning robot.

Abby and Darlene are frozen now, looking at Spike.

The crowd buzzes.

"Quiet," Spike says. And they listen. "Quiet, y'all. I want you to hear every last one of their screams and cries, I want you to hear Jack Jupiter yelling for his momma when I put a bullet in his gut and he's leaking out all over the dirt." He hops down off of the platform, one gun in hand, looking at me, and he says in a softer voice, the southern drawl in full swing. "You really picked the wrong town to mess with, pard."

"Fuck you," I say.

He smiles.

Butch Hazard has his gun pressed against Norm's temple, and even he cracks a smile. It's an odd sight, seeing a man with a gun in hand, blood running from his nose and mouth, smiling. Nightmare-inducing, really.

Spike seems to look past me.

The crowd's quiet lessens. Hushed whispers ruffle through them like the wind through the leaves. I hear someone shout, *"Look out!"*

But as I spin around, it's too late. Sal the mechanic and his buddy, the Broken Kneecap Convict, are on me, driving me to the dirt. I see the door I couldn't close all the way hanging open, cracked enough for two curious zombies to come through.

Damn it.

As my head thumps the ground, I hear Darlene scream.

45

SAL STILL SMELLS LIKE GREASE AND STALE CIGARETTES. His mouth is wide open and I'm trying to block him with my arms crossed into an X, problem is if he bites me, I'm fucked. Plain and simple. I don't have any armor on, my arms are bare in this dingy t-shirt I've been wearing since God knows when.

I'm not ready to go. Not yet.

But I don't know if I really have a choice. My body is betraying me. I am weak.

The mechanic chomps down at my face. Black spit dribbles from his teeth, hangs low right in front of my eyes. The smell is terrible. If a bite doesn't kill me surely the stink will.

He shifts his position, sliding his chest up my arms, sticking his head closer to my face. I turn but can't really go anywhere.

The Convict, grapples at my boot. I feel his teeth clamping on the leather. I kick out, feel the thud of boot hitting meat, and Convict pinwheels his arms and topples over.

The crowd *oohs and ahhs.*

Now all I have to worry about is Sal. His jaw is opening and closing, teeth gnashing against each other.

"Stop it!" Darlene screams.

From the corner of my eye I see her lurch forward to come after me, but Spike says, "Move again, wench, and I blow your tits off."

She freezes on the spot.

Abby grabs her, holds her in place.

I hadn't noticed before, but I'm screaming, grunting in pain. My bullet wound is on fire. The muscles in my arms are screaming. I am dying. My body is giving out.

The Mechanic presses down on me. He is lumpy and hard. There are knots beneath his coveralls. Hard knots of bone, of...

Metal?

I let my arms give out. The Mechanic crashes down on me.

A sharp burst of pain explodes through my sternum as one particular knot in this zombie's chest bites into my flesh.

What is it?

Spike is laughing. "Look at him struggle. The great

Jack Jupiter, Carnivore and murderer! Struggling like a common man. See? He's just like the rest of us. He ain't no one special! They're all like this. We don't have to fear 'em."

No, not Carnivores, but you have to fear me, is what I want to say but can't.

The crowd explodes into cheers.

Then Herb's voice is running through my mind, drowning out the sounds of the crowd and the screams and the snarls of the zombie.

Salvation lies within the heart.

Another of his cryptic messages that shouldn't mean anything, but I'm grasping at straws (zombie limbs) here.

Salvation lies within the heart.

Remember Sal!

Sal...Salvador...Salvation.

It's a long shot, but what the hell? I got nothing else to lose. I'm dead either way, and I don't want to just keel over and die without a fight like the old Jack Jupiter would've done. No, I'm Johnny Deadslayer now.

I press my hand up against Sal's chest. He is soft, mushy beneath his coveralls. My hands find his collar and I rip it open.

The shape of a gun pulsates from this mechanic's rotten flesh, right where a heart that no longer beats lies. There are jagged and loose stitches around this patch of sewn flesh. Dried, crusty blood, too.

I can't believe it, but I almost can.

Salvation lies within the heart, Jacky! Herb's voice again.

I am like a man on the top floor of a burning skyscraper, looking out at the certain doom below me, while flames lick at my back and push me toward the open window. I don't want to jump, but there's no other choice. I might survive the leap. I might not. I certainly won't survive the flames and being buried beneath thousands of pounds of rubble and ash.

I *have* to plunge into the unknown, or I have to die.

It's that simple. It's that complicated.

With my left forearm pressing into Sal's neck, his slobber spraying and dripping all over my face, his rattles momentarily choked off, I take my right hand and peel away the skin like some demented Christmas present.

I am plunging.

I am falling off of the skyscraper. The blazing heat from the flames is disappearing. Smoke is no longer filling my lungs. I am tasting the sweet air of freedom.

Of *salvation*.

The stitches pop easily enough and Sal doesn't even notice I'm tearing him apart.

"Stop it!" Darlene says. "You fucking rat bastard, stop it!"

I am still screaming, but I no longer hear my own screams. I just feel the burning in my lungs, the serrated blade grinding against my vocal cords like a violin's bow hitting frayed strings.

What I see first is a plastic container. A good, old Ziplock bag meant for leftovers and keeping food fresh.

Herb, you clever son of a bitch. I could kiss—

Thunder claps twice.

Red rain showers my face.

Bits of mushy gray brain find their way into my mouth.

I am coughing. My ears are ringing. A shadow consumes me, eclipsing the floodlights like the moon blocks the sun.

It's Spike. His gun is smoking and he smiles.

Salvador the mechanic is lifeless on top of me. His dead weight pins me to the ground and my hand digs deeper and deeper into his open chest. I am screaming in pain. My wrist has broken or at least suffered a really bad sprain.

"I think you've had enough, Jupiter," Spike says. His voice is calm and steady, neither a Brooklyn accent or the clichéd cowboy one. I hated both, but at least they don't upset me to the very core of my existence like this unwavering voice of insanity does. He chuckles. It's a humorless chuckle, then he says, "Time to put you out of your misery, Jack."

He levels the big revolver a mere three feet from my face.

46

IF HE PULLS THE TRIGGER, IT'S NOT GOING TO BE PRETTY.

Cold blood drains onto the dirt behind my head, dampening my hair.

I am Johnny Deadslayer I am Johnny Deadslayer I am Johnny Deadslayer goes off in my mind over and over again.

Salvation lies within the heart.

Darlene screams.

"Jack, no!" Norm says, his voice muffled and pained.

Abby is sobbing.

The crowd is revving up again. *"We want blood! We want blood! Kill him! Kill him!"*

"Guess we won't get to that shoot-off after all," Spike says.

I smile, tasting my own blood on my teeth. "That's

where you're wrong," I say. And my cramped hand inside of Salvador's chest wraps around the warm gun, plastic baggie and all.

I slide my middle finger on the trigger and lift up with all my might. A momentary look of confusion passes Spike's features, then like the quick-draw cowboy he is, he finally notices what I'm doing.

The smile vanishes.

I pull the trigger with my middle finger — a final *fuck you* to this psychotic bastard. And as the gun claps and my eyes blink with the sound, I see Tony and Brian Richards, I see Herb, and Darlene and Norm and Abby, their pained faces in my mind all easing.

A hole the size of a plate rips through Salvador's back in a spray of black blood and white shards of spinal cord. I feel the thunder shake my body, hear the sound of the crack reverberating through the quiet of the stunned crowd.

The bullet hits Spike like a bolt of lighting.

But it's not a clean hit, at least that's not what it looks like at first. A chunk of his face is missing. From the ear to the lower left of his jaw is practically blown out. He now looks more like a zombie, no longer the rootinest, tootinest cowboy this side of the Mississippi. His left eye hangs from its socket. His hair singes, maybe even it's on fire. And the thing I like the most — yeah, this is good — is that his stupid cowboy hat is gone, blown off somewhere behind him.

Spike stands there stunned, rocking on his heels. This goes on for a long moment. His hand comes up to his face, his free hand. Most of his fingers disappear into the hole. When he pulls them out, they are slick and dripping with scarlet blood.

He screams.

It is the scream of a man who is covered in flames, of one who is dying.

The crowd no longer chants. They are as quiet, as stunned as Spike, as me, Darlene, Norm, Abby... as everyone.

With his right hand, Spike brings up the gun. It is shaking and it looks as if he can barely hold its weight, let alone pull the trigger.

"Think that's funny?" he says, the words coming out slurred and painful. His tongue moves like the surface of a pond catching a light breeze. "Think you can shoot me? *Me!*"

The one good eye has gone into red alert mode. No longer does that eye say murder. It's somehow moved past that point to darker intentions if that's even possible.

I try to squirm my way out from under the lifeless Salvador, but I'm having no such luck.

"Think it's funny? I'll...I'll show you what's funny, you no-good, dirty-rotten, pig — " Spike is cut off. But he is not cut off by another shot or zombie attack.

No. None of that.

Spike is cut off by death.

He falls down to the dirt in a growing pool of his own blood. Dead.

Dead.

Dead.

And I fall with him, my head thudding against the dirt hard enough to send a field of black stars across my vision. The gun skitters away to my right.

I might be half-dead with a leaking zombie on top of me, but I've never felt so good in my life.

47

THE CROWD IS STIRRING NOW, REALIZING THEIR GREAT — and late — leader is dead. They start to move. Where they are going, I have no idea.

"He's dead! He's dead!" someone in the stands shouts. I can't tell if it's joy, surprise, triumph, or even shock, but right at this moment, I don't care. They don't have guns. They aren't zombies. I am alive and Spike isn't.

"Jack!" Darlene says.

She runs over to me — well, more like limps. Her face is wet and shiny, I reckon it's sweat *and* tears. Come to think of it, I'm pretty sweaty, too. Florida is hot as hell as it is, and even hotter with a dead guy laying on top of you. I might be crying, too. I won't lie. Seeing Darlene, seeing her in one piece, still alive, with a faint smile on her face just makes me sob. So yeah, I'll admit it.

Darlene says, "Oh, Jack, oh, my God!" She kneels down in the dirt and blood, then as our eyes lock together like two lovers who've not seen each other in years, she says, "That was fucking awesome!"

The crowd seems to be growing restless, buzzing back and forth, trying to find a way out like birds trapped in a one-window room. Or, like chickens with their heads cut off. They are lost without their leader.

I look back to Darlene and smile. "Can't take credit for it. All of that goes to Herb, that son of a gun — "

"Jack! Watch out!" Abby shouts.

Darlene snaps her head toward her, and as she does, I see Butch Hazard, aiming his Desert Eagle at Darlene and I. Some of the crowd behind, those not worried about getting out of this crumbling safe haven, stop and start to point. A few cheer. A few jeer.

The faint chant of, *"More blood! We want more blood!"* comes from the stands.

Butch has Norm in a headlock. He is squeezing so tight, Norm's eyes bulge out and his face is a beat red which is shocking compared to the ashy gray hue his skin had taken on as of late. But the worst thing is Norm isn't fighting back or even struggling. I'd never thought I'd see the day where my hard-ass, big brother stops fighting.

It's fitting that the day I see it is the day I die.

Darlene is slowly shifting herself closer to me. I can see how rigid she is out of the corner of my eyes. There is one soldier still standing. He is the fatter one. His face is bloody and he looks like a man who's frayed rope of sanity has snapped, too. He holds his weapon on Abby and watches us from the corner of his eyes.

"Impressive," Butch says. Two streams of blood run down from his nostrils. When he talks, red mist sprays the air. "I'm glad you did it. Someone had to do it." He shivers. "Wouldn't be right if it was me."

"When did you ever care about what's right or wrong?" I ask.

Butch smiles. "Good point."

The chrome of the Desert Eagle does not sparkle anymore. Its shine is muted by dirt and blood.

"I hate to have to thank you this way, Jack Jupiter, but I'd never feel safe knowing you are out there somewhere, looking for a place to call home. A place like this."

"I wouldn't stay here if you paid me," I say.

Butch shrugs, but I almost can't tell since he is so tense.

I'm trying to form my plan, my last stand. I've not come this far to lose anyone else, to die at the hands of a grunt after I've slain the Black Hat.

I want nothing more right now than to at least be able to stand and shield Darlene, to protect her.

"You won't have to," Butch says. "You won't have to stay anywhere."

My eyes scan the situation. There's the emptying

bleachers and the few stragglers who have not yet had their appetite for death and destruction satisfied. There's the soldier with the AR15 trained on Abby. The dead Spike. Salvador on the bottom half of me, pinning me to the dirt with his cold blood spilling out. Me, half-propped up and in pain. The beaten female soldier. What's left of the zombies Spike shot.

Butch grins, and lets go of Norm, who drops to all fours in a heap. He kicks Norm in the ass, sending him sprawling out in the blood-muddy dirt. "Line up, all of y — "

I shove with all my might at the zombie on top of me, my eyes bulging worse than Norm's were. The pain in my body is unreal, but it's nothing as bad as getting shot. I manage to lift Salvador off of my legs enough to wiggle out from beneath him. The slick blood and guts also helps. I try to ignore that, though.

Butch shoots two times with the Desert Eagle. Two earth-shattering cracks. I am hit with a spray of rotten meat.

I think I've been shot.

Darlene is screaming.

It's all a blur.

My left hand closes around the pistol I used to shoot Spike with it. It's still warm and shiny with Salvador's innards, but I get a good enough grip on it to point, aim, and fire once.

The thunderclap from the muzzle is deafening.

The first slug takes Butch in the middle of the chest.

He hardly seems to notice. But his knees give out on him and the Desert Eagle in his hand falls to the dirt.

A blossoming red rose shows through Butch's dirty shirt. He looks down, his hand coming up to touch the blood, then he looks up at me. He does not look like he is in pain. He is smiling, perhaps relieved.

"Nice shot," he says, tottering then falling face-first into the dirt.

"Thanks," I say, "but I was aiming for your head."

He doesn't answer.

He is dead.

The soldier with his gun trained on Abby moves the aim toward me, but I'm faster and he knows this.

I don't pull the trigger, though. I'm shaking. My blood pumping with adrenaline, my brain craving the kill, wanting to feel the power that comes from the gun just one more time.

I refrain.

"Don't be stupid, man. Drop your gun and get the hell out of here. Don't die for these bastards. Don't die for this piece of shit place," I say instead of killing him.

His face goes pale, his eyes go wide, and he drops the AR15, turns tail, and runs — well, actually waddles.

I push myself up from the dirt. There are no more jeers or cheers from the crowd. They look at me the same way they'd look at a sleeping lion trapped in a zoo exhibit — with fear, awe, wonder.

I look back, and they start to disperse. Some even make like the last fat soldier and bolt.

When they're all gone or no longer looking at me, I let the menacing act drop and almost fall over. I can't help it. Darlene is on me faster than I was on the gun, steadying me, whispering into my ear, "Jack, I love you I love you oh my god I love you. Jack, are you okay? Jack? Jack..."

I'm so beat and tired and scared, I almost can't say it back.

But I do.

"I love you, too." And then I collapse.

48

We are like *The Breakfast Club*: an army jock, a pretty girl, a basket case, and a nerd. Except, imagine the Breakfast Club covered in dirt and zombie guts, sporting bruises like they're this summer's latest fashion trend.

It takes me a minute to come to, but now I'm standing straight up, mostly on my own. Darlene's arms are still around me.

Outside the arena, the citizens are going crazy. I look up and see black, greasy smoke drifting in the air. Not so far away, I hear a car horn blaring.

"We gotta get out of here," I say.

Abby looks at me and nods. It looks painful for her to do it.

I turn to Darlene. Her face is dotted with blood,

blood that I don't think belongs to her, and she's still the most beautiful girl in the world. I kiss her.

"C'mon," I say, heading over to Norm. He's almost out cold, but he's alive. Thank God.

"Norm," I say. He slowly turns his head up to me. His eyes are bloodshot, his neck is purple and growing blacker. To put it as simply as possible, he looks like shit. Still, my older brother, a man who I hated for leaving me to rot in a dead town almost fifteen years ago, manages to smile at me.

And I smile back, extending my hand. He takes it and all three of us — Abby, Darlene, and I — help him up.

We limp out of the arena, the sounds of chaos all around us, a little beaten, a little broken, but otherwise whole. I don't give Spike or Butch Hazard a last look over my shoulder. They don't deserve that.

Let them rot. Let them *all* rot.

49

SEEING THE STREETS BUZZ WITH PEOPLE ALMOST GIVES me a heart attack. It's been a long time since I've seen streets this full. I wish it were under better circumstances, though. People have taken to busting out windows, flipping carts full of stale bread and rotten fruit, and lighting various buildings on fire. I'm reminded of Woodhaven. That is the tightrope Eden is balancing on.

What's even odder is that all of these people who are ruining this place have smiles on their faces, like they're glad to be free from the metal walls holding them in. I almost grab at a man who's running around with his shirt off screaming, "FREEDOM! FREEDOM!" and tell him that sometimes freedom isn't all that nice, especially when you don't know when your next meal will come, but I don't. I barely have the energy. Besides, let them find out on their own.

I'm done with Eden.

We're all done with Eden. There are bigger things on the horizon. Surviving. Thriving. Maybe even a cure.

"Herb," I say to Darlene. "We gotta get Herb."

She looks at me crooked, people streaming all around us, screaming, shouting, jumping for joy. "I don't know — "

"We have to. If it wasn't for him, I'd be dead...we all would." My voice is harsh, but it gets my point across. I don't think they understand so I pull the cure card. "He knows about a cure. He knows a way to beat this thing. Him and the Doctor — "

"Oh, Doctor Klein? He was such a nice man," Darlene says.

"Yeah," I say. "He knows about something in D.C."

They eye me like I'm going crazy. I have to rally the troops.

"Don't you want the world to go back to the way it was? Don't you want to have to quit worrying about zombies and demented cowboys and crazy army people? I sure as fuck do. C'mon, we've survived this long, we can help Herb and the Doctor."

Norm nods. He looks proud, proud to call me his younger brother. "I'm in," he says. "I'm sick of aimlessly wandering. I want to do some good."

"Yeah," Abby says. "He's right."

"Darlene?" I ask, looking at her, trying not to notice the chaos slowly budding beyond her.

"I can't say no," she says. "You know I always want to help, but Jack we are barely alive ourselves."

"I'm always alive as long as I'm with you," I say.

She breaks into a smile.

"Oh, barf," Norm says, chuckling.

Darlene rolls her eyes. "Fine, Jack...as if I could really say no to you."

I turn to my brother who has been here the longest and ask, "Norm, you know where the dungeon is?"

He looks up at me a little less dazed, his soldier instincts kicking in. "Yeah," he says. "I know where it is. Follow me." Somehow, he hobbles faster, and we follow. Rescue Operation: Herb Walker is a go, then it's on to Rescue Operation: Planet Earth.

The dungeon isn't as much of a dungeon as it is a space-themed restaurant that never was. I can tell, even with the signs on the outside of the brick facade ripped off, leaving a dark ghost of the words that were once hanging there. *Space* something. What really gives it away is the domed roof. I'm instantly reminded of being a seventh-grader again and going on a class field trip to Cleveland and seeing the Great Lakes Science Center's planetarium.

"There it is," Norm says. He is hunched over, out of breath despite the walk being about two minutes from the Arena. It's a hot night, and the flames have been spreading. It's almost impossible not to feel the heat.

A burst of gunfire erupts into the air not far from where we are standing. I clench up and put my body in front of Darlene. She squeezes me.

"I'm okay," she says. "I'm tougher now. You've taught me well, Jack Jupiter."

I smile. As much as I want to believe it, I can't. Deep down, when someone has a gun pointed in your face or a knife at your neck, no one is tough.

We hear more gunfire and see the afterimage of the bursts in the night air. I see a man in Butch Hazard's soldier's camouflaged outfit. Three regular people are on him. I can tell they're regular people by the way their clothes hang off of their wiry and emaciated bodies. You'd think this soldier could take them, AR15 and all, but he doesn't. The Edenites are on him like zombies on us, except they don't eat him. Instead, they just stomp him, grab his rifle, club him with it over and over again. I don't see the blood flying, but I swear I hear it pattering the concrete, even from all the way back here.

It's gruesome. Demented. I'd almost prefer to

watch a horde of zombies on him instead. At least the zombies don't know right from wrong.

Almost.

The urge to get out of here intensifies.

Abby opens the door to the dungeon, snapping us all out of this trance we must've been in. The door squeaks its rusty hinges, and next thing I know we are plunging into total darkness, me in the lead. As I walk, I keep thinking to myself this is where Spike did his fucked up experiments on zombies. There's probably an entire horde down here.

There's an iron door a little ways down a corridor. The window is blacked out with electrical tape. NO ENTRY is scrawled on the metal with red paint. I put my hand up to the rest of the group trailing behind me. "I'll check it out," I whisper.

I go down the hall and grab the handle. For what seems like the millionth time in my life, I am met with a gun to my face.

Except it's exactly the gun I'm looking for.

"Jacky!" Herb says. He lowers the pistol, and grabs me, squeezing me with all his strength — which is a lot, trust me. "Jacky! It worked! It worked! I heard them saying that mean old Mr. Spike was dead, but I didn't believe it."

My words are choked out of me. "Herb, p-p-please let me go."

His eyes go wide. "Oh, I'm sorry. I'm just so excited to see you, Jacky!"

I rub at my ribs. "Norm, Darlene, and Abby are outside," I say, pointing to the door.

"They are?" He smiles like a kid on Christmas morning. "Tell them to come in! Guys come in!" His voice is loud.

The door cracks. It's Darlene. She is radiant in the dim light, smiling. "Herb," she says. "I'm so glad to see you!"

He runs over to her, hugs her, but this time it's a little more gentle than when he hugged me. He does the same to Abby, but Norm, he backs off, recognizing his injuries.

"Where'd you get a gun, Herb?" Darlene asks.

He looks down at the pistol, which is probably huge in my hands but looks like a water pistol in his, like it's a slithering snake. "Doc Klein gave it to me. He came and busted me out of that nasty prison cell. He hurt the guard real bad. Not killed him just beat him up and he said to me, 'Herb, things are going to get very bad. I am leaving for D.C. Spike is gone and that may be good, but now we are weak. If we don't get out, the Carnies are going to get us. I'm going to do some good in this world. You can come with me. Time is short. Do you understand, Herbert?' I nodded my head real slow. I understood, all right. I understood real well. But I said no, I was gonna come look for Jacky and you, Darlene. All of you. You're my friends."

Darlene pats him on his arm, and he smiles again.

"When I told Doc Klein that I was gonna go out there and look for you and he said, 'God bless' just like my auntie used to before every meal — 'Dear lord God Jesus, bless us. Bless this food,' but me and the Doc weren't eating. No, we wasn't. Then I heard the guns and smelled the fire and came back and hid in the dungeon because I was scared..." he looks down at his feet. "Real scared. Said I'd go out there when I didn't hear it no more."

"Well I'm glad you stayed put, Herb," I say. "We're all here. A little beat up but here, and now we can get the h-e-double hockey sticks outta here!"

The momentary sadness passes and he beams again. "I knew we'd find each other, Jacky! I just knew it!"

"Guys," Abby says from somewhere across the room. I can barely see her shrouded in the shadows. "Guys, we hit the jackpot."

I hobble over there, Darlene, Herb, and Norm in Herb's arms following me. Abby stands in front of a large supply closet, stacked with medicines: Oxycodone, prednisone, Moxifloxacine, Diazepam. There's jugs of purified water. Boxes of food. Bandages. First-aid kits. You name it.

"Grab it all," I say, knowing we have a long road

ahead of us. "Everyone grab as much as we can and let's get the hell out of here."

Herb claps a hand over his mouth. "Aw, Jack said a bad word!"

I just shake my head, smiling.

In a warehouse not far from the lab, are rows and rows of cars. Most of them have been stripped for parts, and others have been taken and driven by the smarter of the Edenites — I know this because of the car sized hole in the fallen garage door and the skid marks on the gray floor.

When I see the warehouse and how ransacked it looks, I almost lose hope. There is not much choice left, but the flames are getting hotter and soon, if we don't get the hell out of here, we are going to burn.

Herb points to a minivan sitting on two flats. The body is rusty, it's baby blue paint peeling and flaky, but it's big and roomy.

"Where are the keys?" I ask.

"Gonna need them," Norm says, then he wheezes a burst of painful laughter. Back in the lab, he downed a bottle of ibuprofen and took some other pain pill I couldn't even pronounce. And there's one thing I know about drugs you can't pronounce: They usually have the trippiest side-effects.

More gunfire rips through the air in the middle of the abandoned amusement park, but it's far off, muted by distance.

"Keys are in there," Herb says. He points to a metal box on the wall. Its cover already hangs open. The keys inside of it sway back and forth as if a ghostly breeze is in the warehouse. "I'll go get 'em. Number 19," he says, pointing to the 19 written in white paint on the corner of the windshield.

"That's if they're still in there," I say under my breath.

Abby hears me and chuckles. "Nobody wanted that piece of shit," she says, smiling. It looks foreign on her swollen face.

Herb comes back beaming like always, the tiny keys dangling from his oversized pinky.

"Wanna drive?" I ask.

The smile vanishes. "I-I never drove before. Not since my auntie — "

"Herb, it's all right," Norm says. "I'll help you. Just none of us are fit to drive right now. You gotta help us out a little while longer."

"Yeah," Darlene says, "You're our hero, Herb."

He smiles again. "I'll do my best."

As he walks by me, I clap him on the back.

We load up the van, file in, and buckle our seat belts. The van's engine sputters for the first couple turns, but roars to life on the third try. It *is* the charm, I guess.

Herb guns it out of the warehouse, the flat rubber *slap-slapping* on the desolate and destroyed streets of the abandoned amusement park.

By the time we pull through Eden's broken gates, our headlights washing over stooped and starving — yet otherwise happy — former citizens, the flames have begun to paint the sky with their orange glow. Part of the roller coaster whines, creaks, then falls over. It's chaos. Maelstrom. Another version of *The End.*

No one tries to stop us. No one jumps on the car. Most of them have weapons, probably having broken into one of the various lockups. But no one shoots at us, either.

Herb drives. He hasn't driven in years. Norm is in the front seat, guiding him, telling him when to brake and when to speed up. It's just how you'd imagine a worried father teaching his son to drive. But Herb does fine.

"Herb, how would you like to go to D.C., and see your friend Doctor Klein?" I ask.

His eyes get huge in the rearview mirror. "Would I?" he shouts, then sighs, shaking his head. "But I don't know how to get there."

"Don't worry, Herb, we'll find our way," I say.

He smiles, nods at me, and focuses on the open road.

Abby, Darlene, and I are in the backseat. The trunk is stuffed full of medicinal supplies, non-perishable foods, and as many stray weapons as we could find. We are set for the foreseeable future.

I glance up at the dashboard and see the gas tank is half-full, not half-empty — that's just the kind of guy I am right now.

We are heading north to find Doctor Klein, to save the world. We can do it. I know we can.

As the trees go by in a dark blur and the distance between us and Eden grows, I hear Darlene's soft snores. Not long after her snores taper off, I fall into the blackness of sleep. And I dream of our wedding again, but this time it's not gruesome. The only people in attendance are the ones I care about: Norm, Abby, Herb, and my future wife.

We kiss when the priest tells us to kiss, long and deep. I wake up shortly after, and I kiss her for real. It's beautiful, and in a world full of death, it's life.

ABOUT THE AUTHOR

Flint Maxwell lives in Ohio, where the skies are always gray and the sports teams are consistently disappointing. He loves *Star Wars*, basketball, Stephen King novels, and almost anything falling under the category of horror. You can probably find him hanging out with one (or *all*) of his six dogs when he's not writing or watching Netflix.

Get in touch with Flint on Facebook

Made in the USA
Monee, IL
24 February 2021

61271274R00184